RING OF SHAME

Douglas John Knox

Cover Photos: Pixabay.

Cover Design: Douglas John Knox

email: Douglasjohnknox@gmail.com
Twitter: @douglasjohn_k
Facebook: @douglasjohnknox

CONTENTS

RING OF SHAME

It's a January morning and the body of a young woman, shoeless and unsuitably attired for winter, is found dead in the freezing waters of a seaside town's harbour. She has no identification and no one has reported her missing.

Did she jump, or was she pushed? Who is she?

Three days later another young woman's body, similarly dressed, is discovered in a different location. But are the two deaths linked?

Detective Chief Inspector Max Cornell thinks they are and have died for the same reason. But how does he begin the investigation when faced with interference from his superior, no witnesses, clues or evidence.

A gripping crime mystery, set in Newcastle and Northumberland

CHAPTER ONE

Sunday

He'd been to Herrington once before as a child of six or seven. It had been a school outing. Now almost thirty something years later, the place still looked familiar although he doubted if the roundabout in the main street was that old.

Detective Chief Inspector Max Cornell brought his car to a halt alongside a police vehicle parked at the entrance to the harbour. To his left, a row of boarded up brightly coloured kiosks advertised excursions to the Farne Islands.

That school trip had included a visit to the Farne's and he recalled hundreds of seabirds swarming around their heads. Apparently, they do that during the nesting season. There were almost as many rabbits and as a result the turf was bouncy due to their mining activities. He wasn't sure why he remembered all that.

He pulled his six-foot three-inch frame out of his vehicle and retrieved from the rear seat the new anorak he had purchased the previous week.

Today was a day off and he was casually dressed in jeans and sweater, not deeming it

1

necessary to change his clothes on getting the call out. He hadn't minded being disturbed at home. There was no one there waiting for him to return.

He glanced at his watch. It was ten o'clock on a cold, grey, stormy Sunday morning in January, and recently promoted DCI Max Cornell stood and looked around to get his bearings.

He could see the white spume on the windblown grey waves beyond the harbour wall and remembered his mother calling them white horses.

White horses?

He locked his car and set off walking in to the harbour through its gate, which closed at nine thirty in the evenings according to the notice bolted to it.

Two uniformed police officers approached him from the pier.

'DCI Cornell?' asked the elder one.

'I am,' replied the Head of Northumbria's Murder Investigation Team, displaying his ID.

'Inspector Shaun Lambert and PC Green, sir, from Alnwick.'

Although the two men had never met, Cornell was aware that Lambert was the officer in charge of Alnwick police station, in whose jurisdiction they currently were.

Lambert was almost totally bald, short in stature and prone to weight gain. The tall constable looked fit, as if he worked out and played football three times a week. The three men shook hands.

'So, you have a body,' stated Cornell.

'Along the pier here, sir. About fifty metres,' answered PC Green.

Cornell spotted the pathologist's tent on the pier and followed the two officers from Alnwick towards it.

It was low tide and Cornell could smell the exposed seaweed on the outer side of the harbour wall.

Above the sound of the wind, there was the cry of seagulls, a noise synonymous with all UK coastal towns. Some gulls were squabbling in the calm water of the harbour over something thrown overboard by a boatman.

Police tape was stretched across the pier, the area guarded by a uniformed police constable who lifted the tape to allow the trio access. Inevitably and despite the weather, several people, ghoulish or just plain curious, had congregated at the tape.

The tent flapping in the wind was precariously perched near the edge of the pier beside a boat moored to the harbour wall. Once a fishing vessel, it was now converted to take passengers.

Looking around the harbour, Cornell could see that most of the vessels were the same. Lobsters aside, and there were a number of pots stacked neatly on the piers, it appeared Herrington had long since been a fishing village.

'The body is female, sir,' said PC Green as

they approached the pathologist's tent. 'Found at around seven thirty this morning floating face down by that boat over there, sir; "The Island Rover."'

Green pointed to a boat moored at right angles to them on another pier.

'Who found her?' Cornell asked Inspector Lambert.

'The boat owner of this vessel, sir, "The Sea Angel." He had been here since six working below deck and didn't notice the body until later when he switched his deck lights on. He and two other boatmen lifted her out and brought her up these steps. They tried AR, sir, but she was well dead.'

'Pathologist been here long?' Cornell asked.

'About half an hour, sir,' answered Lambert.

'Who is it?' asked Cornell.

'Mabel Wainwright. Have you met her before?'

'Yes, I have.'

Cornell donned surgeon's gloves and blue plastic shoe covers offered by PC Green, then entered the tent. He was about to announce his identity.

'Who's that?' demanded the kneeling pathologist whose back was towards him. She was dressed in a white throwaway overall and instructing a similarly dressed male assistant armed with a large camera, where to take pictures of a prostrate female body.

'Detective Chief Inspector Max Cornell,

Senior Investigating Officer, Murder Investigation Team, Northumbria,' said the intruder standing his ground.

'That's one hell of a mouthful, chief inspector,' the kneeling figure proffered. 'Doctor Mabel Wainwright, forensics pathology.' She turned towards him to acknowledge his presence. 'But we've met before, haven't we? You remember my assistant, Tom Mawson.'

She stood up beside Cornell. She was almost a foot shorter than him, the "one size fits all" overall making her appear much plumper that she actually was. Her non made up face, framed by the attached hood, did little for her attraction.

'Pleased to meet you again, Doctor Mabel Wainwright. So, what have we got?'

'Female, late teens early twenties, I would guess. Dead for around ten to twelve hours.'

'Has she been in the water for that length of time, doctor?'

'Probably, chief inspector, I think she drowned.'

'Did she do that herself?'

'Well, she has bruises to her back and arms, which could have resulted from a struggle and she has a busted lip which could have been from a punch. But there are no obvious signs of blunt force trauma to her head or body.'

'Any ID?' asked the detective.

'No,' replied the pathologist. 'She doesn't appear to have a coat either. Nor does she have shoes, jewellery, a phone, no car keys, no nothing.'

'Is she a murder victim, doctor?'

'I don't know that, chief inspector. That's your department.'

Cornell bent forward to look at the body. She was blonde and a pretty girl he decided, despite her bruised mouth and pale-yellow discolouration from the water. Her eye sockets were dark, one looked darker than the other.

'That a black eye, doctor?'

'Well spotted. It could be and probably is, but not necessarily so. The eye sockets would become dark and hooded in cold water. One eye may be more so than the other. There is one thing, although you men wouldn't notice.'

'What's that?'

'She is either well off, or has a good provider. Those are expensive designer clothes she's wearing, right down to her underwear. Clothes for going out in, or entertaining.'

'I look forward to your report, doctor. I'll send my DC to the autopsy.'

'Squeamish, chief inspector?'

'No, doctor. I've been at many an autopsy. I've got the T shirt, but if I never see another, it will be too soon and one too many.'

***

Cornell removed his gloves and shoe covers and handed them back to Constable Green. He explained the pathologist's preliminary deductions to the officers.

'Murder, sir?' queried Inspector Lambert.

'Have to wait for the autopsy report. Looks like she drowned, but we don't know whether she jumped or was pushed. Nor do we have an ID. Would it be worth putting a diver down there, inspector?'

Cornell pointed to the area where the body had been retrieved. 'See if we can find a phone, car keys or something.'

'Have to search the whole harbour, sir. She would have drifted around with the tides. Cost a fortune.'

Cornell shook his head. He looked around at the houses that overlooked the harbour. In the immediate vicinity, there were the typical stone homes of fishermen, but more modern and less appealing houses had been built beyond the harbour area.

Cornell turned his attention to the harbour itself. A number of vessels had been lifted out of the water for maintenance and repainting during the winter. He had a thought which he put to the inspector.

'Any chance she came in on a boat and was dumped here?'

'Extremely doubtful, sir. It would have been dark and the boat would have needed lights to navigate with and they would have been seen, but I will check it out with the harbour master.'

'If you would,' agreed Cornell. 'Who was the

first plod on the scene?'

'PC Hargreaves, sir. He's the local bobby, knows everybody in Herrington. Do you want to speak to him?'

Cornell nodded. Lambert shouted for Hargreaves. A tall, plump, grey haired and noticeably near the end of his career police officer strode over to where they were standing. Lambert introduced them.

'Have you seen the young lady's body?' Cornell asked him.

'Yes, sir, when I first arrived on the scene, but I've not seen her in these parts before. I don't think she's local,' said the officer, anticipating the chief inspector's next question.

'Can you vouch for the vessel owners who found her and brought her up on to the pier?'

'On my life, sir. Known them since childhood, sir. Went to school with all of them.'

'OK. So, where do kids this girl's age go to in Herrington on a Saturday night?'

'Good question, sir. There's no night club in Herrington and the two pubs here don't really cater for the young, sir, so they head off to Alnwick, mostly. Some get as far as Morpeth.'

'Thought Herrington was a holiday town, officer.'

'A holiday village, sir. It's hardly a town.'

'What about the caravan parks?' asked Cornell.

'There are two parks in Herrington. They

have their own entertainment, bingo mainly. But not much of that at this time of year and hardly an attraction to young folk. This girl was most likely attending a private party of some description, sir.'

'What about CCTV?'

'Sir, this is Herrington. Nothing in the main street. They have it in the pubs and the entrances to the caravan parks, but I doubt if they even have it switched on in January.'

'Thank you, PC Hargreaves, you've been very helpful.'

The officer, knowing he hadn't really contributed very much at all, re-joined his colleagues.

The coroner's vehicle reversed on to the pier and the body, now bagged, was placed in the rear. The pathologist's tent was dismantled by the assistant.

Cornell addressed Inspector Lambert.

'Check with the caravan parks, hotels and pubs to see if anyone knows this girl, or saw her yesterday, or last night. See if all parked cars in the near vicinity can be accounted for. There's little else we can do until we establish the girl's identity and cause of death. Do you have enough officers?'

'I'll call some of them in, sir. They'll jump at the overtime.'

'Fine. I'll be at home this afternoon. Here's my mobile number. Call me if you get anything.'

Probably isn't a murder. More likely a suicide?

But jumping into icy cold water? And where are her outer clothes? Her phone? Her watch? Does she live local? If not, where has she come from? And what was she doing in Herrington in January? Who was she?

CHAPTER TWO

Sunday evening

Maximillian Royston Brent-Cornell was the only child of Captain Jason and Elizabeth Brent-Cornell and once having left school and home at the same time, he dropped his middle name, lost the first part of his double-barrelled surname and shortened his first name to Max.

He felt better for doing so. It was like having a huge burden lifted from his shoulders. No longer would people scoff and mock his ridiculously long appellation, for which he blamed his father.

Cornell never got on with his father who was too preoccupied with army life to bother with his son, or devote much time to his wife for that matter.

Despite that, the family followed Captain Jason Brent-Cornell to live in Hertfordshire so as he could be nearer to his headquarters and thus further his army career.

Both Max and his mother hated the area and as soon as Max left school he departed for London. He found work on a building site until he was old enough to join the Metropolitan police.

Shortly after his escape to London, his father was killed in action in some remote conflict overseas. His mother inherited a lump sum and an army pension and returned to live in relative affluence in her native north east England where she resumed her career as a teacher of infant children.

Max, meanwhile, progressed steadily through various uniformed roles until eventually becoming a detective where, blessed with an excellent memory and the ability to think laterally, he became an effective problem solver.

His promotion to sergeant found him in special branch and shortly after, in counter terrorism working alongside the security services.

***

Max Cornell had come a long way since then. Having lived a dangerous life on special assignment in the northwest of the country for a number of years, he eventually found himself as a DCI in the relative tranquillity, by comparison, in the North East of England.

And now jogging along Whitley Bay promenade on a raw but fine Sunday evening, he was merely killing time until he went to bed. He knew once he got there, he would lie awake for hours considering all the connotations as to what happened to the girl found dead that morning in Herrington Harbour. He knew that, because it always happened to him when there was a new crime to investigate.

It was such a frustration not knowing who the Herrington body was, where she had come from and what she was doing in Herrington. Inspector Lambert had obviously not been able to identify the girl, as Cornell had received no call from him that afternoon.

He wished he had someone with whom he could talk to about the death. Apart from his mother, he had no friends or near relatives to go and visit or to come and visit him, and his mother's occasional stop off was more to do with her making sure he was looking after her property, rather than a social call.

She constantly told him he should have a partner, or at least a pet dog, but Max would argue history and that he and partners were not a good mix, and he had never owned a pet dog to relate to.

He would never admit to being lonely, but he was.

Reaching the causeway to St. Mary's lighthouse, he about turned and began the journey home. The tide was out and on impulse he ran across the beach to the waterline where the sand was more compact to continue his run.

CHAPTER THREE

Monday

Laura Donaldson was a detective constable with three and a half years' service. She joined the Northumbria Police' two-year graduate trainee detective program direct from university at the age of twenty-two.

Traditionally, police officers spend years in uniform before becoming a detective and the fact she had circumvented the practice, caused a great deal of animosity amongst the front-line police officers.

However, Donaldson didn't seem affected by the caustic comments regarding her status and gender and when confronted, she always responded in kind.

In the short time she had been an operational detective, she had served under three chief inspectors. The first was a gruff elderly sexist who didn't think women made good detectives, the second, a temporary stand in was in her opinion, not up to the job and the third was Max Cornell.

Since arriving at Newcastle, he had already

earned her respect. He treated her the same as her male colleagues, didn't seem to be disposed to anger and had a great sense of humour. His laid-back and easy-going attitude was in sharp contrast to the chief superintendent's brusque approach.

***

By the time Chief Inspector Cornell had driven in the slush through the morning rush hour traffic to the police station, emptying his screen washer in the process, Detective Constable Laura Donaldson had already marked up a whiteboard headed with the name, "Jane Doe."

A photo of the dead girl sent over by the forensics laboratory was Blu Tacked beneath it.

Cornell took off his coat, threw it across a vacant desk and addressed the young detective.

'Do we know when the autopsy is being done?'

'This afternoon, sir.'

'You been to one yet, Donaldson?'

'No, sir. Can't say it's high on my "to do" list, but it's my turn to attend one.'

'First time for everything and it's easy after the first one unless a body is badly decomposed. That can be a little rough.'

'Thank you, sir. I'll look forward to it,' she responded, pulling a face.

'Any news from Alnwick about her identity? Lambert didn't get back to me yesterday.'

'Inspector Lambert rang in before, sir, but

only to say that he hasn't discovered anything about the dead girl yet, although he still has some places to contact.'

'What about missing persons,' commanded Cornell.

'Nothing, sir. No missing person reported over the weekend. The last one was a week ago and he turned up, sir.'

Cornell looked around at his team of four officers, led by a sergeant.

'This is what we have so far,' Cornell addressed his crew. 'Female, late teens early twenties, well off, found dead and floating in the harbour at Herrington yesterday morning. Inadequately dressed for the time of year, no shoes or coat, no ID, no phone, no car keys. Any thoughts?'

'How do you know she was well off, sir?' asked DC Ian Dennison.

'Good question,' answered Cornell. 'I wouldn't have known if the pathologist hadn't told me. Apparently, she was wearing rather expensive designer clothes.'

'So, she's been at a party, sir,' added Dennison, smiling from ear to ear at his contribution.

'That's a distinct possibility,' Cornell answered, adding "party?" to the whiteboard.

'Sir,' chirped DC David Watkins, 'she didn't have any shoes on, so, did she leave them wherever she was at? lose them on the way to the harbour?

or lose them in the water?'

Cornell wrote "where are her shoes?" on the whiteboard. Sergeant Bob Harvey joined the discussion. A respected long serving officer approaching retirement, Harvey had been married for twenty-five years to a detective sergeant in the drug squad. He always did things by the book and expected everyone else, including his superiors, to do the same. Harvey was blessed with a good sense of humour which Cornell appreciated and he was one of the best organisers Cornell had ever come across. His theories were always worth listening to.

'If she left her shoes behind,' Harvey queried, 'it would suggest to me that she had to leave wherever she was in a hurry. I cannot see her taking her shoes off once she was outside.'

'Unless she was wearing high heels and took them off in order to run from something,' interjected Donaldson.

'So, where are they?' countered Harvey. 'No shoes have been found anywhere in the harbour or in the nearby streets.'

'No outer clothes have been found either, so I favour she left them somewhere,' said Cornell. 'I agree with Sergeant Harvey, I think she had to leave wherever she was in a hurry.'

'Which could mean she was chased,' furthered Watkins.

'And chased all the way to the harbour and shoved in,' suggested Dennison.

'Quite,' said Cornell. 'But we have no evidence of that whatsoever. Indeed, the lass could have been suffering mentally and decided to end it all by jumping into the freezing cold water of Herrington Harbour.'

'But you don't really believe that, do you, sir?' suggested Harvey.

'I'm unconvinced, let's put it that way. What we need is a place where she was at during the evening. It would also help if we could confirm PC Hargreaves' belief that she wasn't a Herrington lass. Not least, knowing who the hell she was.'

There was quiet in the incident room as the team racked their brains.

'I think she could be a student,' Laura Donaldson announced suddenly.

'Why do you think that?' queried Bob Harvey.

'Right age. It's what well off teenagers do, isn't it? Go to university?'

'Good one, Donaldson. I think that is worth pursuing,' exclaimed Cornell. 'Bob, get on to Newcastle University now. Send them her photograph. Get somebody over there if they recognise it. If they don't, try Northumbria and Durham universities. I'll be in my office.'

***

Cornell retrieved his coat and left the incident room. Back in his office and sat at his desk, he wondered why a young woman, little more than a girl, would voluntarily be in Herrington Harbour on a Saturday night in January dressed for a night out in June.

Was she local? Was she with someone? Probably, but who? Why hasn't this someone contacted the police? Where's my daughter? my wife? my partner? It's now been more than twenty-four hours since she was found.

His office door opened abruptly and Chief Superintendent Mark Braithwaite, commander of Northumbria Police northern area, poked his head in.

His hair, slicked back with the modern-day equivalent of Brylcreem, matching the unremitting shiny, almost slimy, facial five o'clock shadow on his chin. Cornell had this image of him being kissed and the other party sticking to him.

'Identified that girl yet?' enquired the chief superintendent.

'No, sir, not yet,' replied Cornell.

'Cause of death?'

'Not yet established; probably drowning. Waiting for autopsy report.'

'If she drowned then it's got to be suicide.'

'Possibly, unless she was pushed, sir.'

'She could have swum, couldn't she? All kids can swim nowadays,' stated the chief superintendent.

'If we haven't got an identity by tonight, sir, we can give a small press conference and ask for assistance from the public.'

'No. Not for a suicide. Someone will come forward sooner or later.'

Braithwaite then left, closing the door louder than was necessary. Cornell did not want another run in with his superior, recalling the recent dressing down he had received for using too much overtime to trap a drug dealer. The positive result hadn't mattered.

Chief Superintendent Braithwaite did not like Cornell. He had not been involved in the chief inspector's appointment and that rankled. The former DCI had retired and it was Braithwaite's job to recruit the next, or so he thought. He was far from happy when the chief constable announced the successor without any consultation with him.

Braithwaite, Cornell had decided, unlike most senior police officers, did not like the limelight and was keen to keep out of the way of the media. And he was a dinosaur; the old brigade, disinclined to accept change and move into the twenty first century.

Cornell had sat through Braithwaite's meetings and listened to the boring reporting back from headquarters. He had watched his inspector colleagues trying to impress by making notes of reported crime figures and wondered what the hell they did with them.

Up from last year, down from the year before, averaging out over ten years. Who the hell cares? What's more important is what is happening today.

***

'Can't think of where else to look, chief inspector,' said Inspector Shaun Lambert from Alnwick, telephoning in later that morning. 'Spent last night doing the pubs and hotels with PC Green. No one saw the girl on Saturday night, nor have they seen her before. I've had a team out checking the B&B's today. Nothing so far. Caravan parks are empty of people. Can't find a car for her either.'

'Anyone hesitant or reluctant to talk to you?' asked Cornell.

'No, sir. Everybody we spoke to was most co-operative.'

'So, are we able to say this girl was definitely not a Herrington resident?'

'I think so, sir, otherwise PC Hargreaves would have known her. Hardly a visiting tourist either, not at this time of year.'

'So, why was she in Herrington? Visiting a relative, perhaps?'

'Could be, but surely a relative would have come forward if she'd left without her shoes and outer clothes . Even if there'd been an argument.'

"Donaldson thinks she could be a student, Shaun, and we are following that up. I thought a press conference to ask the public for help was a positive thing to do, but the chief super wouldn't have it.'

'He's not noted for appearing before the

press, chief inspector,' answered Lambert. 'Sir, I'm not going to be available for the next couple of days. The MP for this constituency arrived here at the weekend to visit his flock and I've got to arrange security for him this week while he's on official business.'

'Who came up with that bright idea?' asked Cornell.

'Chief Superintendent Braithwaite's orders, sir. Sergeant Makepeace and PC Green will be here if you need them.'

'OK, we'll speak again when you are free of the political world.'

***

'The pathologist will email her report first thing tomorrow, sir,' said DC Donaldson later that day on her return from the lab. 'And she confirms that death was due to drowning. There are also lacerations on the girl's feet suggesting she ran on a hard surface without shoes at some stage before she died.'

'But what was she running from or to? Had she taken any drugs?' asked Cornell.

'Some traces of cocaine in her system, but not enough to cause death or impede her capacity, sir.'

'Thanks, Laura.'

'Sir,' Harvey called out from his desk.

'Yes, Bob?' Cornell deferred to his sergeant.

'Newcastle University think they recognise

the photo of the dead girl we emailed them, so I've sent Dennison over there.'

Chief Inspector Cornell stood in front of the whiteboard with a coffee while Donaldson wrote up the information from the post mortem.

'So, she ran from something or someone. Couldn't have been far. Not in bare feet on such a cold night.'

'Dennison has an ID, sir,' shouted Bob Harvey taking a call at his desk.

'Great, put the call on speaker, Bob.'

Dennison's voice came over loud and clear.

'A lecturer recognised the photograph. Her name is Janice Whittaker and she's a second-year student, at least she was until last November when she dropped out.'

'Dropped out for what reason?' asked Cornell.

'She never gave one, sir. I spoke to her tutor who said she became preoccupied with something other than learning, but she wouldn't say what. Lost interest in her subject and just stopped attending lectures. According to the university's personnel records she lived with her parents. They used to live in Gosforth, but moved to Morpeth about four months ago. Her father is a well-regarded barrister, who can be verbally abusive, apparently.'

'Good work, Ian,' acknowledged Harvey. 'What's the address of the parents?'

Dennison read out the address and Bob

Harvey wrote it down.

'Well, we'd better go see him,' declared Cornell. 'Donaldson, you're with me. Bring your abuse deflector. Sergeant Harvey, let the lab know we have a possible ID for the Herrington death. Will arrange identification.'

Cornell would normally have given the job of informing parents of their child's death to his sergeant, but there was something about this case which intrigued him.

So, the dead girl was a student. Still need to find out what she was doing in Herrington and who, if anyone, she was with. Hopefully, her parents will oblige.

CHAPTER FOUR

Monday evening

The chief inspector began to ease off the accelerator as he and his detective constable approached Morpeth from the A1 in the darkness of a wet and cold January evening.

The Whittaker family home was on a new housing development on the northern outskirts of Morpeth, the postcode unknown to his satnav and not yet available on Google Maps. A phone call to traffic had given them a rough direction.

'That's it, sir,' Donaldson pointed through the wipers sweeping rhythmically across the windscreen at the brightly lit entrance of a plush housing estate. 'The site hasn't been here very long, sir. Built for the exceedingly rich of Newcastle and Northumberland.'

'I thought Darras Hall fulfilled that demand.'

'It does, sir, but Darras Hall is full. This is an overspill, you might say.'

Cornell drove slowly along a rough, pot holed road yet to receive its final layer of tarmac.

Large new houses were situated behind ornate brick walls, many entrances not showing any identification. Then one house displayed a number from which they were able to calculate their destination.

Cornell turned into a drive a good fifty metres long which led up to a house with Georgian pillars, like the old plantation houses of America's deep south. A Mercedes S class stood on the drive in front of the garage and Cornell thought that if that was his car, it would be inside the garage in this weather. Light from a downstairs room exposed the front garden as still in the process of being landscaped.

As they approached the door a high wattage security light flashed on from above. Inside the porch a CCTV camera was placed to record those attending, its small censor light flickering red.

Donaldson rang the doorbell. The chime of a classical Beethoven riff could be heard from inside.

'Definitely have a better class of council house in Morpeth,' pronounced Cornell facetiously.

Donaldson had to stifle a laugh, remembering the purpose of their visit.

The door was opened by a slight man of around five feet ten, thinning hair, bespectacled, sporting a light-coloured waistcoat and a spotted bow tie. Cornell would have placed him around fifty to fifty-five.

Both police officers produced their warrant cards.

'Mr Paul Whittaker?' enquired Cornell. 'I

am Detective Chief Inspector Cornell and this is Detective Constable Donaldson. May we come in, sir?'

'Why? What is this about?'

Despite the challenge, Cornell had the distinct impression the visit was not unexpected. He could also feel the welcoming heat from inside the house and dearly wanted to be out of the cold.

'It's not something we can discuss on your doorstep, sir.'

'Well, if you must. Follow me.'

Whittaker led them through a hall into a large lounge with windows on two sides and non-curtained French doors in the rear wall, which looked out on to an illuminated, but empty garden.

A plainly dressed woman sitting off to one side was introduced as Mrs Joan Whittaker. She smiled and nodded at the visitors but remained seated, seemingly disinclined to offer refreshment to her guests.

The barrister sat down on what was clearly his chair and motioned his two visitors to avail themselves of a four-seater black leather settee opposite.

'Mr and Mrs Whittaker,' began Cornell, 'when was the last time you saw or heard from your daughter?'

'Which one?' Whittaker asked.

'Janice.'

'Sometime last week. Why?' answered Whittaker, rather sternly.

'Could you be a bit more precise, sir,' chimed Donaldson.

'Young lady, my eldest daughter is twenty years of age. I do not check on her every move.'

'Janice live at home, did she?' interjected Cornell. 'We learned she dropped out of university in late November.'

'And why would you need to learn that?' demanded Whittaker, seemingly irritated with the questioning and the intrusion into his family issues.

'Mr Whittaker, did your daughter, Janice, live at home?'

'Yes,' he retorted loudly. 'She lived at home most of the time except at weekends and don't ask me where she went to, or stayed at, or what she got up to, because she didn't tell me.'

Cornell turned his attention to the lady of the house. She was constantly sniffing and looked as if she had a bad cold, or even the flu.

'Can you help, madam? Can you recall when you last saw your daughter, Janice?' Cornell asked.

'It was Friday. I last saw her on Friday afternoon,' she said in a slightly slurred voice between sniffs. 'She was going away for the weekend like she always did. I don't know where she went to.'

'Is this your daughter, sir?' Donaldson took a photo of the dead girl from her briefcase and placed it on the coffee table in front of the barrister.

Whittaker stared at the photo, his eyes wide in recognition and shock that the girl in the picture, his daughter, was so obviously dead.

Mrs Whittaker got to her feet, somewhat unsteadily, and came and looked at the photograph.

'Oh, my God! No! What has happened to her?' she cried, stumbling backwards into her chair.

'Mr Whittaker, Mrs Whittaker,' said Cornell, 'there is no easy way to say this, but I'm afraid the person of whom this is a photograph, was found dead yesterday morning.'

Whittaker went rigid, staring at the picture. There was a cry of anguish from his wife, who immediately began to weep and sniff together.

Cornell, surprised that Whittaker had no words of solace for his wife, asked them both if they would like a cup of tea, which Constable Donaldson would make. Whittaker refused for both himself and his wife.

'A glass of water then?'

'No,' emphasised Whittaker.

'You have other children, Mr Whittaker?' prompted Cornell, asking questions of the father rather than the mother.

'Yes, a daughter, Edith. She is with her grandparents at the moment. She is not involved with this.'

'Not involved with what, Mr Whittaker?' asked Cornell.

'Don't try to catch me out, chief inspector,' snapped Whittaker. 'I do this for a living. I'm a QC you know.'

'I know, Mr Whittaker,' said Cornell. 'That's why I'm surprised you haven't asked how your daughter died.'

'Err, yes. It's the shock. How did she die, chief inspector?'

'She was found at Herrington, Mr Whittaker. She had drowned in the harbour.'

'Are you saying she committed suicide, chief inspector?'

'That's a possibility, but it is only supposition at the moment,' replied Cornell. 'Do you have any idea why Janice would be in Herrington on Saturday night, Mr Whittaker?'

'How would I know?'

'Did she have many friends?' questioned Cornell.

'Again, chief inspector, I did not require my daughter to provide me with a list of her acquaintances, or keep a log book of her activities for that matter.'

'Did she ever bring any friends home, Mr Whittaker?'

'Occasionally, but I do not know who they were. I cannot remember their names. Is there anything else, chief inspector?'

Cornell glanced at Mrs Whittaker, but she seemed consumed with weeping, sniffing and picking at her fingernails.

'May we see Janice's bedroom, sir?' enquired Donaldson.

Whittaker bristled.

'No, you may not.'

'And why not, Mr Whittaker?' asked Cornell.

'I am not going to have you trample all over my house without a search warrant.'

'OK. You said your daughter Edith is with her grandparents, Mr Whittaker. Is that your parents or your wife's?'

'Why do you want to know that?' asked Whittaker belligerently.

'Because we will need to speak to Edith, and to do that we need to know where her grandparents live,' replied Cornell.

'Why? She has nothing to do with this.'

'Nevertheless, we still need to speak with her,' stipulated Cornell, refraining from again asking Whittaker what she had nothing to do with.

'They are my wife's parents. They are called Harris,' Whittaker offered with much reluctance.

'Do you have their address?'

Cornell looked from one parent to the other.

'Do you have it?' Whittaker demanded of his wife who was still dabbing her red eyes and nose with a tissue. She lifted a handbag from her side and took out an address book. She opened it and turned a few pages offering the contents for Cornell, who stood up, to read.

'Thank you, Mrs Whittaker.'

Cornell returned to the sofa. 'I will need you to come to the morgue and formally identify your daughter. At least one of you.'

Whittaker appeared annoyed at the instruction, but as a lawyer he would know it needed to be done.

'I'll do it,' he said almost angrily.

'It should be done tomorrow,' said Cornell. 'Eleven o'clock. I'll arrange for a police officer to be present. Mrs Whittaker would you like to attend as well?'

'Most certainly not,' retorted Whittaker.

Joan Whittaker's body language suggested she might like to see her daughter for the last time. But she shook her head when Cornell asked her, probably because her husband was looking daggers at her.

Whittaker stood to signify as far as he was concerned, the conversation was over.

'Final question, Mr Whittaker. Does your daughter own a car and have you any idea where it is now?'

'Of course, she owned a car. It was a blue Citroen, but don't ask me what model it was, or its number and no, I haven't a clue where it is.'

Cornell stood too, said goodbye and led his colleague out of the house to their vehicle.

Driving back to Newcastle, Cornell asked his detective constable what she thought of Paul Whitaker QC.

'What a horrible man. He is so awful.

No wonder the younger daughter left home. Surprised Janice didn't, although she may have been staying in university accommodation before she dropped out. Did you notice, sir, that Whittaker never once referred to her by her first name?'

'I did, and I'm sure I got a whiff of alcohol, possibly sherry, when I leant over to read Mrs Whittaker's address book,' commented Cornell. 'I could be wrong, but I think Paul Whittaker was acting. I think he already knew Janice was dead. I think the reason he didn't ask how she died was because he already knew. He was also a bit too quick to conclude she had committed suicide. There's something not right here and I cannot figure out what it is.'

'Where do the grandparents live?' asked Donaldson.

'Low Fell, Gateshead. They are called Harris, but I think we'll leave that visit until tomorrow. We've done enough today, don't you think?'

OK, victim identified. Still don't know whether suicide or murder. Parents informed, but father and mother's attitudes strange, if not suspicious. Father jumped to the conclusion his daughter had committed suicide, same as Braithwaite. Umm!

CHAPTER FIVE

Tuesday

Chief Inspector Cornell took another swig of coffee and decided he couldn't drink anymore. He placed the cup and saucer containing the remaining anaemic concoction on his chief superintendent's desk.

Both he and his superior were reading the pathologist's preliminary report for Janice Whittaker.

'This just confirms she committed suicide,' said the chief superintendent.

'Well, it confirms she drowned, but she could have been pushed in. The pathologist doesn't give a view as to whether she was murdered,' countered Cornell.

'She wouldn't, but there is no evidence a crime has been committed here at all.'

'I think she ran from something. Something bad, sir. Bad enough to make her run in her bare feet and leave all her belongings behind. Bad enough, that if she wasn't pushed, she felt it necessary to voluntarily jump into icy cold water to escape her pursuer.'

'Without evidence to the contrary we can still chalk it off as suicide. The coroner isn't going to argue,' said the chief superintendent, rubbing his chin which appeared to need shaving again despite it only being mid-morning.

'Nonetheless,' persisted Cornell, 'she received some physical punishment prior to her death. A punch or a slap. Not enough to kill her, but could have been instrumental in her running, or how she came to be in the water. Unfortunately, forensics drew a blank on tracing any DNA.'

'So, what's your next move, chief inspector? I don't want Paul Whittaker and his wife hassled further. They have enough to contend with after losing their daughter.'

So, Whittaker's been in touch then?

'I will try to see the grandparents today, sir, and hopefully the younger sister, to see if they can throw any light on the proceedings.'

'And afterwards, chief inspector, unless you have any evidence that Miss Janice Whittaker was murdered, close this case as a suicide. I can't afford to waste anymore man hours on a suicide.'

Cornell returned to the incident room.

'Where is Sergeant Harvey?' he asked.

'Got a call from the lab, sir,' answered Laura Donaldson. 'Paul Whittaker turned up at the morgue at ten o'clock, demanding to see his daughter's body. Dr Wainwright was not best pleased as he was causing aggravation, so Sarge went across to calm things down.'

'But his appointment wasn't until eleven. I had arranged for a uniform to be present.'

'Having met the man yesterday, sir, I'm not really surprised.'

At that precise moment Sergeant Bob Harvey returned, bursting into the incident room and throwing his coat and scarf in the direction of the coat hooks.

'That bloody man. Thinks he's God's gift to justice. Apparently, he just turned up and demanded he see his daughter's body there and then. Kept saying he was a QC and would have Doctor Wainwright's job if she didn't see to it. Have to say mind, she didn't hold back. Something like, she didn't care if he was the Lord Chief Justice, Attorney General and Master of the Rolls bundled together, she was not going to acquiesce to his threats. Maybe not as pleasant as that. However, I saw he was not going to be appeased, so in the interest of peace and tranquillity, I suggested we got on with the procedure to get him out of the building. Doc Wainwright reluctantly agreed.'

'How did he appear when he saw Janice?' asked Cornell.

'Didn't bat an eye, sir,' answered Harvey. 'I asked if the body was that of his daughter, Janice Whittaker. He mumbled a "yes" then turned and walked away.'

'Takes all sorts. Laura, this afternoon I want you to run a background check on Paul Whittaker. Bob, take Dennison and meet up with

PC Hargreaves in Herrington and look for Janice's car. It has to be somewhere. We've got the number from Swansea. Then try and figure out where she ran from on Saturday night. Knock on some doors if you have to. Someone knows something about her. David, you and I are going to see the Harris family later on this afternoon.'

'Can I drive, Sarge?' asked an enthusiastic DC Ian Dennison of Bob Harvey. Dennison was an ex-traffic cop and the youngest member of the team; cocky, if not cheeky on occasions. Notorious for crashing and totalling two police vehicles, the last one, a week-old BMW, as recently as two months ago. As a result, Dennison had become available to Cornell who felt sorry for him, as no other department believed they could afford his destructiveness.

'No, you bloody cannot,' retorted Harvey. 'You just sit still in the passenger seat and move nowt but your eyes.'

***

Cornell accompanied by DC David Watkins drove over the Tyne Bridge en route to Low Fell.

Watkins was an ex-beat bobby in his late twenties. Never flustered and calm in the face of adversity.

Cornell reflected that at one time, due to the senseless height restriction application rule, Watkins would not have been tall enough to join the police force. Despite his small stature, Cornell had witnessed him face down and calmly disarm three drunken, beer bottle wielding Newcastle United supporters, and not felt the need to interfere.

No mean feat in this part of the world and it was this action that earned him a place on the murder investigation team, although DCI Cornell himself would have difficulty in explaining the correlation.

Watkins' wife insisted that her husband be called by his full first name, and those who had met her, complied fully.

The weather was bright and sunny for a change, although frost still adorned the areas of ground where the weak winter sun had not shone.

The forecast was not good however, Cornell recalling the weather reporter that morning saying, "make the most of today as snow is on its way."

On reaching Low Fell, Cornell turned left up a slight hill, the sat nav spitting out instructions.

'That's it,' said Watkins, pointing to the end house in a street of semi's.

They parked outside a gate beyond which the path took them through a neat and tidy garden, still in the shade and white with frost.

Their knock on the front door was answered by a smart, well-dressed lady who would probably be in her late sixties, or early seventies.

'Mrs Harris?' asked Watkins.

'Yes.'

'Mrs Harris, I'm Detective Constable Watkins and this is Detective Chief Inspector Cornell. May we come in please?'

'It's not about Edith, is it?' the lady asked, her face portraying anguish.

'No, ma'am, it's not about Edith,' answered Watkins, 'but we would like to speak with her. May we come in?'

'Yes, yes, come in.'

The lady stood aside and held the door for the officers to enter the house. 'Edith is at school, I'm afraid. She finishes at half past three and is home around four. My husband has just come back from the shops. I'll ask him to join us.'

Cornell glanced at his watch. It had just turned three thirty. They were led into a cosy lounge, a welcoming artificial coal fire providing sufficient warmth. 'Can I get you both a cup of tea?' asked Mrs Harris.

'That would be nice,' Cornell accepted.

In a matter of minutes Mrs Harris returned with a tea tray, accompanied with a small plate of custard creams.

Mr Harris followed her into the room and was introduced. He removed his outer jacket and placed it neatly over the back of a chair. In his waistcoat, collar and tie he looked like he could have been a school master.

'It's about Janice then, is it?' questioned Mrs Harris, shuffling on to a settee alongside her husband.

'Why do you think that, ma'am?' queried Cornell.

'Oh, that child has always been a worry to us. She always did what she liked and got away with it. But she is clever, chief inspector. She was always in trouble at school, but always came top of her class. A teacher's nightmare. If you ask me…'

'Mrs Harris,' Cornell put his hands up to stop her talking, 'and Mr Harris, I'm so sorry. I'm afraid Janice is dead.'

'Oh my God!' exclaimed Mrs Harris, raising her hands to her mouth, then grabbing her husband's hands. 'Richard, oh, Richard!' she sobbed.

The man put his arm around his wife's shoulders.

'Are you sure she's dead? How did she die? Has she been identified?' he asked. 'I'm sorry, I'm asking too many questions at once.'

'Her father identified her body this morning. Janice was found in Herrington Harbour on Sunday morning. She had drowned, but we are still investigating the circumstances of her death. This is a photograph taken shortly after she was found.'

Watkins showed them the photo. Both Harris's, flinched at the sight of their dead granddaughter.

'Yes, that's her. But Herrington? What on earth was she doing in Herrington?' asked Mr Harris.

'We don't know, Mr Harris,' answered Cornell. 'We are trying to trace her movements on Saturday night and drawing a blank on why she was in Herrington. Do you know if she had any friends there?'

'I don't. I don't suppose her parents would know either. Edith might.'

'Why do you think her parents would not know, sir?' asked Cornell.

'It's a long story, but suffice to say we have not spoken to our daughter and son-in-law for quite a while.'

'I'm sorry about that. Can you tell me why?'

'Our son-in-law is a sanctimonious, arrogant, supercilious, egotistical bastard.' Harris turned to his wife and patting her hand said, 'Sorry my dear.'

Cornell almost asked, "don't you like him then?" but wisely refrained.

Harris continued. 'He treats his family and everyone else atrociously. He caused his wife, our daughter, to drink more than she should and did not provide a happy home for our grandchildren. Fortunately, Edith had the good sense to leave and come to us before he could damage her permanently. But Janice, I'm afraid, had a mind of her own and did her own thing. In my view, by remaining at home she eventually became damaged.'

'When was the last time you saw Janice?' asked Watkins.

'It would have been about three weeks ago, just before Christmas. She came to visit but only wanted to talk to Edith. They had an argument. I don't know what it was about. Then Janice was downright rude towards her grandmother, so we told her to leave. I feel guilty now.'

'Do you think Janice was murdered, chief inspector?' asked Mrs Harris.

'I honestly don't know, Mrs Harris. There are issues surrounding her death that I'm not happy with, such as why she was not wearing a coat or shoes and why she was in Herrington in the first place. Do you think she could have taken her own life, Mrs Harris?'

'No, not Janice. Definitely not. She was too strong willed. I would stake my life on it.'

'I'm home,' called a young female voice from the hallway accompanied by what could have been school bags being dropped on to a tiled floor. The lounge door burst open and a girl aged about fifteen or sixteen entered the room.

'Edith,' Mrs Harris said in response to the girl's surprise at company. 'Edith, sit down, my dear. I'm afraid we have some bad news for you.'

Looking quizzically at the visitors, Edith took a seat and Mrs Harris explained to her in precise terms of the demise of her elder sister. Cornell was grateful for that. The grandmother did it far better and with more empathy than he could have.

Edith was upset. She looked downward with

her hands clasped, but she didn't cry.

Cornell waited for the news to sink in, then took up the questioning.

'Edith, is it alright to ask you some questions? If it's not, we can come back another time.'

The girl continued looking down but nodded her ascent.

'Edith, when was the last time you saw Janice?'

'Sometime in December,' she answered without emotion.

'Was it a social visit?'

Edith shrugged.

'What did you talk about?'

'I can't remember.'

'But you had an argument, dear. It upset you,' declared Mrs Harris.

Edith shook her head.

Cornell decided she didn't want to talk about that, so took a different tack.

'Did you know if Janice had many friends, Edith?'

'She had one good friend at university. I met her once, but I can't remember her name.'

'Do you think they would have gone to Herrington for any particular reason?'

Edith shrugged again.

'Do you know if they ever went anywhere together?' asked Cornell, who felt if Edith knew anything at all, he was going to have to drag it out of her.

'I don't know. But she may have put something in her diary.'

'She kept a diary?' asked Cornell enthusiastically.

'Yes. She always kept it locked and became angry if I ever went near it.'

A few questions later, Cornell deduced that Edith hated her father with a vengeance, believing him to be quite mad. She loved her mother, but received little support from her. She was very happy living with her grandparents.

***

'Unfortunately, we didn't get a great deal of information from the Harris household,' Cornell informed Donaldson when he and Watkins returned to the station in the early evening. 'Have you found anything on our friend Whittaker?'

'Interesting,' his only female detective returned. 'Whittaker was a practising barrister and fairly successful until about eight months ago. Doesn't appear to have worked since.'

'Do we know what happened then?'

'He just stopped accepting briefs and eventually dropped out. His partners, not very forthcoming, would only say he was the leading defence counsel in a big trial but he was not the same person after it.'

'Must have lost a case badly.'

'No, sir. He didn't lose a case, he won one.

A big one. I've looked it up. Whittaker acted for a local mobster, William Tierney, known affectionately as Buffalo Bill because he used to wear a cowboy hat all the time. Suspected of importing girls from Eastern Europe and using them as sex workers. He was not beyond murder and it was on a murder charge that he was in court. The CPS threw the book at him, sir, but none of it stuck.'

'Who was the investigating officer?'

'Chief Superintendent Braithwaite, sir.'

At that moment Sergeant Harvey rang in from Herrington.

'How did you get on, Bob?' asked Cornell.

'Not great, sir. There is the hotel overlooking the harbour and although it was busy on Saturday night, there was no party. The same with the pub across the street, which just doesn't lend itself to private parties anyway. PC Hargreaves and his colleagues have done house to house on the surrounding buildings with the same negative result.'

'Any sign of Janice's car in Herrington?'

'Hargreaves tells me there are three Citroen C3 owners in Herrington. All their cars are accounted for. No sign of Janice's.'

'Must be parked up somewhere,' suggested Cornell.

'Sir, there are not many garages in Herrington. The older houses have no room for them. So folk park their cars on the street outside their homes, mostly. Some new houses have garages, but Hargreaves has checked them all out.'

'OK. I'll ask traffic to keep an eye out for a blue Citroen C3, Northumberland and County Durham. '

Cornell ended the call and turned to his detectives to relay the information from Lambert. 'I think we should call it a day, DC Donaldson. You and Watkins get yourselves home. See you tomorrow.'

***

Cornell poured himself another beer. He should be relaxing in front of his television, but following his conversation with Harvey, he had rung an angry Paul Whittaker who was not going to allow a police search of his property without a warrant.

Cornell had not mentioned the diary to him. If there was one, he was in no doubt Whittaker would find it and depending what was in it, dispose of it. No, he would have to get a warrant as Whittaker had demanded.

He drank the beer, had two more then went to sleep in his chair during the highlights of a FA cup replay, waking up to the weather forecast that informed him of imminent snow storms in the North East of England.

So, Janice kept a diary and had a good friend. Father an obnoxious barrister, won a case he perhaps shouldn't have, then dropped out. Why? Superintendent Braithwaite lead detective in that case. Were the two somehow linked? Something is not right. What is it?

CHAPTER SIX

Wednesday

Cornell sat back in his office chair with his feet on the desk, and pondered. He pondered over a father's apathy towards his daughter's death and what had caused the death. The father's reaction had been too quick to conclude it must have been suicide.

He pondered over a possible connection between a barrister, a police superintendent, a mobster and a twenty-year-old girl.

The phone rang bringing Cornell back to the present.

'DCI Cornell,' he answered.

'Sir, it's Lambert here, Alnwick. Sir, we have another body.'

'Bloody hell! What do you mean, another body? A dead body?'

'A girl, sir. Same age group as the Herrington girl. No coat, phone, shoes, no obvious way of how she got here.'

'Where's here, Shaun?'

'Sorry, sir. On the moorland above Cragside.'

'I've heard of Cragside, Shaun, but I haven't a

clue where it is.'

'In Northumberland, sir. Take the A697 from the A1north. After Longframlington, take second left to Rothbury. You will see us on the left, high up on the moors. About a thirty mile trip from Newcastle.'

'OK, Shaun. I'm on my way. But I thought you were babysitting an MP?'

'My sergeant is at the moment, sir. I'm relieving him after I hand this murder over to you.'

'Pathologist been called?'

'Yes, sir. Rang them just before you, sir, and sir...,'

'What?'

'Bring a good coat, sir. It's bloody freezing up here,' adding, 'and your wellies; it's snowing like hell.'

Cornell had his thick anorak and kept gloves and wellingtons in his car boot for cold and water emergencies.

He hesitated for a moment wondering whether he should tell Braithwaite where he was going, then decided not to.

He looked through his glass petition office wall to see if Donaldson was in. She was.

'Laura,' opening his door and calling across the room, 'you are with me. And bring your wellies, crampons and oxygen.'

'Where are we going, sir?' she asked.

'Inspector Lambert has another body on

49

the moors north of Cragside, although from his description it's more like the north face of the Eiger. A girl's body has been found, same age as Janice.'

'Oh, no!' responded Donaldson.

'What do you mean?'

'I'll tell you in the car, sir.'

Once having picked their way through the snow and slush afflicted traffic and joined the A1 north, Donaldson spoke up.

'You recall Edith had told you that Janice had a friend, sir? A good friend by all accounts. I contacted the university this morning, sir, and they confirmed the friendship. The two girls were on the same course. There were others in their circle, but none as close as those two.'

'And you think this body we are going to see could be this close friend?' asked Cornell.

'It's distinctly possible,' replied Donaldson. 'The friend's name is Margaret Whitfield, from Shotley Bridge, near Consett, County Durham. The university was about to contact her parents as she hadn't returned from the Christmas break. Unlike Janice, Margaret hadn't dropped out of university, but her attendances and attention in lectures had become erratic.'

The sat nav advised them to take the A697 slip road towards Coldstream at the next left. After about twelve miles and two villages, they turned left where the ground rose quickly in front of them and the snow had begun to lie on the road.

The sat nav informed them they were nine hundred feet above sea level but the land to the left of them rose sharply for what must have been another three hundred feet.

'There they are,' said Donaldson, pointing left towards the top of the hill. Cornell could barely make out two vehicles and a group of people through the snow, which was falling at an acute angle due to strong breeze. The pathologist's grey square tent was almost invisible.

Cornell parked his vehicle on the side of the main road, not wishing to risk getting it stuck on the slushy path leading up the hill. The cold wind hit them immediately they got out of the car.

'Bloody hell,' said Cornell, reaching for his anorak from the rear seat. 'Lambert wasn't kidding. It is bloody freezing up here.'

He and Donaldson now suitably clad, set off walking up the slope in the tracks left by the police and forensics vehicles. They bent forward into the wind towards the small assemblage and tent. Police tape had been stretched in a square around the tent, although it hardly seemed necessary.

Cornell stood and looked around him. Where they were seemed to be the highest point of the immediate area. The ground to the right fell away into a valley that must have stretched for miles across to the Cheviot Hills which were invisible through the shroud of falling snow.

Inspector Lambert approached, flapping his arms round himself in an attempt to keep warm.

'This sorts the men out from the boys, sir. It's minus seven up here,' he said as Cornell and Donaldson stepped off the hard packed track onto the snow topped springy heather which made walking in a straight line almost impossible.

'So, what have we got here?' asked the chief inspector.

'Dead girl, sir. No coat, no ID, just like the Herrington lass, but we think this one's definitely been murdered.'

Cornell, with difficulty, put disposable blue plastic shoe covers on over the feet of his wellingtons and pushed back the flap on the tent.

'We meet again, doctor.'

He introduced himself to the kneeling pathologist, who was dressed in white throw away overalls, just as on the last occasion they'd met.

'And so soon. Hello, chief inspector,' she answered, then pointed to the body. 'Female, late teens, early twenties, strangulation is the probable cause of death. See the marks around her neck?'

Cornell bent over the girl, a brunette, her face made up, but smudged by the weather and possibly physical abuse. He saw the clearly visible red marks on the throat, highlighted by the surrounding frosted flesh.

'How long has she been dead, doctor?'

'Difficult to tell with the cold, which would delay body deterioration, but I would say between twenty-four and thirty-six hours, certainly no more than that. I can't be more specific until I examine her fully.'

'That's like a day after Janice Whittaker died. I hear you had a run in with her father yesterday.'

'Paul Whittaker? Thoroughly obnoxious man. Been cross examined by him on a number of occasions, although to be fair, not for a while. I never liked him and I like him even less after yesterday.'

'We think Janice and this girl were friends,' Cornell interjected.

'You think there is a connection with their deaths, chief inspector? Miss Whittaker wasn't strangled or suffocated like this one. Of course, if she hadn't run to her death, she may well have been. And this one is also wearing top brand designer clothes.'

'The way both girls were dressed, doctor, and if this girl is who we believe it to be, suggests to me there was some connection with their deaths.'

'You have a name for this girl, chief inspector? She has no ID on her either.'

'Subject to positive identification, we think she is a Margaret Whitfield. We have her address from the university and will contact the parents when we finish here.'

'OK, let the lab know when they will be coming to identify her,' requested the pathologist.

'Can you tell if she was murdered on this spot or brought here, doctor?'

'Again, chief inspector, difficult to tell. If

there are any tracks, they will be under six inches of snow.'

'Hazard a guess?' asked Cornell.

'Most likely dumped here. She was a fit young girl who could have fought back, but there are no defensive marks on her. I think she was killed elsewhere and brought here.'

'If only we knew where "elsewhere" was.'

'Nothing on her to help, chief inspector.'

'Thanks, doctor. Look forward to your report.'

Cornell left the tent.

'Inspector Lambert,' Cornell called out to where Lambert stood talking to Laura Donaldson and PC Green. 'Who found the body?'

The inspector walked closer towards Cornell and dug out his notebook, turning a couple of pages.

'A Mr Albert Henshaw, sir. Lives in that smallholding down there.'

Lambert pointed to a cottage and farm buildings in the distance on the other side of the road. 'He was walking his dog up here early this morning. Says it was his dog that found her.'

'Hasn't he got enough walks on his side of the road? Why on earth would he want to walk up here in this weather? Is he a suspect, Shaun?'

"I would doubt it, sir. Seems like a gentle, lonely old man to me. But I could be wrong. He is expecting us to call on him to get his statement.'

'OK. Donaldson and I will do that. Any car

tracks up here?'

'No, sir. It would have to have been a 4x4 if there were any, but in any case, the snow will have covered them, and you tend not to leave tracks on heather, sir.'

'OK. Those houses next to Henshaw's down there. Have your officers call and see if anyone saw anybody, apart from Henshaw that is, up here these last three days. Then you better get back to your security detail before I incur the wrath of Chief Superintendent Braithwaite for keeping you away from such important work.'

Albert Henshaw lived in the end house of four similar detached stone-built dwellings standing on the opposite side of the road to the hill. Henshaw's house differed from the others only because he had several farm buildings at the side and rear of his property.

'Mr Henshaw?' enquired DC Donaldson. 'Chief Inspector Cornell and Detective Constable Donaldson. May we come in?'

'Err, yes,' replied the stooped, elderly, grey haired man who shuffled aside to allow the two police officers, who were kicking snow from their boots, into his home. 'Hope you don't mind the mess,' he added.

There was no mess. The man had gone to some lengths to tidy up having had advance warning of the officers' visit. The room was cosy and warm as a result of the banked-up wood burning fire.

Cornell stood and looked out of the window. It had stopped snowing and a weak sun was trying to shine, enhancing an incredible view across the valley towards the Cheviot Hills.

To the right, a horse poked its head out of a half door of one of the buildings and in front, a number of hens were scratching their way through the trampled snow.

The tea was made. A teapot, cups and saucers, a milk jug and sugar bowl had been set out on a tray and placed on the table.

A border collie which had barked profusely when they had knocked on the door, stood gently wagging his tail at company it was probably unused to.

'I gather it was your dog who found the body, Mr Henshaw,' declared Cornell when they were all seated with their tea.

'Aye, it was. It was Tip here. Sit down, lad,' Henshaw instructed his dog. It did so immediately, between his knees with its back to his master.

'We was out for our mornin' walk, we was. Tip here loves the snow. Runs about in it like a pup. You wouldn't think he was ten years old. Old for a working collie, that is.'

'Why did you walk up that way this morning, Mr Henshaw?' asked Cornell, not wanting the old man to wander off course. 'There must be easier walks for you on this side of the road.'

'We likes to change our walks every day,

don't we lad? and we are not too old to walk up that hill, you know,' their host responded with some indignation. The dog obviously agreed, wagging his tail, or rather thumping the carpet with it from its sedentary position.

'So, can you tell us what you saw this morning, Mr Henshaw?'

'Well, we was walking up near the top, this 'un running around like a mad thing, when he suddenly stops and looks straight ahead, his nose sniffing away like a good 'un. "What's up lad?" I says. "Go see," and he walks off, very warily, for about fifty yards, then stops and starts barking for me. When I gets to him, I sees this poor lass lying in the snow.'

'What did you do then, Mr Henshaw?' asked Cornell.

'Well, I wasn't going to touch her and do that artificial semination business like you see them do on the telly. I could see she was dead. I've seen enough dead animals to know that she was dead. That's alright, isn't it? I'm not going to get into trouble for not doing it, am I?'

'No, Mr Henshaw,' stated Cornell, not daring to look at Donaldson for fear of breaking into hysterics at their host's malapropism. Cornell held his hand to his mouth while he said in a shaking voice, 'the girl had been dead for a couple of days. There was nothing you could have done.'

At this point Laura Donaldson stood, and in an unusually high-pitched voice pumped with stifled emotion said, 'I'll take these,' collecting the empty cups with shaking hands and taking the tea tray of rattling china to the kitchen, closing the door behind her.

Cornell hoped he would not hear her laughing in the other room, as it would start him off. He coughed and cleared his throat.

'So, what did you do then, Mr Henshaw?'

'Well, we ran back down the hill, didn't we, lad? and rang 999. I don't have one of those mobile things. That Inspector Lambert came and I told him about the girl. He told me to stay in the house and not to go up the hill again until everybody had gone.'

'Is there anyone else living with you, Mr Henshaw?' asked Cornell, gradually regaining his composure.

'No, sir. My Maisie died three years ago now. There's just me and Tip here. I have a few cows, some sheep and a couple a' dozen hens and a horse to keep me busy.'

'Mr Henshaw,' asked Cornell, 'have you noticed any strangers around these last two or three days? People walking up the hill, that sort of thing. Strange cars parked nearby?'

The old farmer thought for a while.

'Can't say I've seen anyone up the hill, mister, or any strange cars hereabouts, but there's always cars around that new house they've built along the road.'

'What new house is that?' Cornell asked as

Donaldson, having regained her equanimity, had returned to the room.

'Oh, that monstrosity off on the right, towards Rothbury. Bloody great big house it is. Should have been built from stone like everywhere else around here. Those bricks spoils the landscape, it does. Makes it stick out like a sore thumb. Should never have got plannin' permission. Somebody's taken a back hander there, I reckon. There are always some strangers around that place too, and they come in bloody big expensive cars.'

Having taken a written statement and bid farewell to Mr Henshaw, the two police officers set off on their return to Newcastle. Quiet at first, it was Donaldson who started it. She had her hand across her mouth and every so often her body would convulse.

Cornell was just as bad. Switching the radio on and trying to sing along to songs he didn't know didn't help, and after uttering a stifled snort, Donaldson began to laugh uncontrollably. Cornell only just managed to keep the car in a straight line for the next two minutes as the couple expelled their merriment.

'Should we have perhaps told him the difference between insemination and respiration, sir?'

'No, it would have spoiled his day.'

'Not something we can put up on the whiteboard, though, is it sir?' Donaldson said later.

'Oh, I don't know.'

Another dead girl, but this one definitely murdered. Left on top of a hill where whoever disposed of her body must have felt she would remain unfound for some time. No one reckoned on Albert Henshaw and his dog, Tip. Two bodies, friends, both students. What the hell is going on? If we could read Janice's diary, that might help.

CHAPTER SEVEN

Thursday

Cornell and his team, minus Ian Dennison who was attending the autopsy of the body thought to be Margaret Whitfield, were sitting in front of the whiteboard. The information and photos displayed referred to the two dead girls, but very little information related to evidence leading to a killer.

'Chief Inspector Cornell,' sounded the voice of Chief Superintendent Braithwaite from distance. 'My office, please.'

Cornell followed his superior along the corridor to his office, frustration bordering on anger having been removed from leading a discussion with his team

'Close the door, chief inspector,' retorted Braithwaite.

Cornell did so, but remained standing. 'Chief inspector,' continued the superintendent taking his seat, 'as far as I am concerned, these two deaths are two separate incidents. One girl committed suicide; the other was murdered. Both unrelated. The first case can now be closed. Do I make myself clear?'

'Sir, I believe the two deaths are connected. The two girls were good friends and similarly dressed when they met their deaths within two days of each other.'

'Why are you so obsessed with this Whittaker girl? She took her own life. Case closed.'

Here we go again. About to challenge authority once more.

'Why are you so insistent, sir, on closing a case when there are elements of it that require further investigation?'

'I'll be the judge of that and may I remind you who you are talking to,' retorted Braithwaite with not a little rancour.

'Sir, the two cases are linked. I can't continue a murder enquiry of the later one without investigating the circumstances of the earlier one.'

'Then I will take you off the case, Chief Inspector Cornell.'

Cornell stared at his superintendent in astonishment.

'Then I will present my facts to the chief constable,' he responded.

The chief superintendent's eyes went wide, bulging, and his mouth fell open at the sheer audacity of his subordinate contemplating going over his head.

'Give me one good reason why I shouldn't suspend you, chief inspector,' growled the superintendent.

'That I'm doing my job?'

'How bloody dare you!' the chief superintendent exploded, now having lost his cool. 'Who the bloody hell do you think you are? You come here from Manchester and think you can take over the place! That you can speak how you like to your superiors and that you can disrespect them!'

'I'm not doing any of those things, sir.'

'Then get the hell out of my office and you are off the case!'

'Carry on brainstorming,' Cornell said to his team when he'd left Braithwaite's office, as calmly as his frustration and anger would allow him, adding, 'I'll be missing for about an hour, possibly two.'

'Everything all right, sir?' asked Laura Donaldson who had picked up on the chief inspector's demeanour.

'Could be better, but I'll see you all later.'

Cornell left the station and walked to his car, speed dialling his smart phone as he did so.

The call was answered.

'Put me through to her, please. It's DCI Cornell.'

Several seconds went by then a female voice answered.

'Max, nice to hear from you. What can I do for you?'

'I need to speak with you, ma'am.'

'Braithwaite giving you a hard time?'

'Worse than that, ma'am.'

'Oh dear. I can give you fifteen minutes if you are here in ten.'

'Yes, ma'am. I'll be there.'

Cornell drove the short distance to Wallsend Headquarters, parked his vehicle and made his way upstairs to the offices of the Northumbria police hierarchy.

A female sergeant collected him from reception, knocked on the door of the chief constable's office and hearing her shout "come," ushered him in.

'No time for coffee, Max,' the chief constable said, pointing to a seat on the opposite side of her desk. 'Let's have it.'

'I have two deaths, ma'am. What looks like a suicide in Herrington and a...'

'And a murder near Rothbury.'

'You've heard?'

'Yes. The two connected?'

'I think so, ma'am, yes.'

'But Braithwaite doesn't.'

'I think there's more to it than that, ma'am.'

The chief constable looked at her watch.

'Quickly, I need to be somewhere.'

'The father of the girl who drowned at Herrington is a barrister, Paul Whittaker.'

'I know him,' responded the chief constable. 'A good advocate by all accounts, but a less than pleasant human.'

'Yes, ma'am. But there is something not right about his daughter's death and I'm sure he knows something about it, or in whatever she was involved. Also, because Braithwaite wants the death categorised as a suicide and the case closed, coupled with insisting he does not want Whittaker hassled, makes me suspect that there is some link between them.'

'Oh, Jesus. Don't say anything more.'

'No, ma'am.'

'When you have solved the mystery, come back and see me.'

'Err, Braithwaite's taken me off the case, ma'am.'

'No, he hasn't. And it's Chief Superintendent Braithwaite to you. Goodbye, Max.'

Cornell stood up and left the chief constable's office. As the door closed slowly behind him, he heard her ask her secretary to hold her car and get Chief Superintendent Braithwaite on the phone immediately.

**

The team were still in front of the whiteboard when Cornell returned to the incident room.

'So, what have you got for me?' he asked with enthusiasm.

'Sir,' Laura Donaldson took the lead, 'we think, because of the circumstances surrounding Janice's and Margaret's deaths, but despite the different way and where they died, they are definitely connected.'

'Tell me how.'

'They were of the same age and friends at university. The fact neither had any ID or anything personal on them and were similarly dressed, is significant. One died one day, the other, the next. Too many coincidences, sir. Before they died, something happened to both, probably the same thing and we need to find out what it is.'

'I agree,' said Cornell. 'So, where do we go from here?'

'Sir,' said Watkins, 'if the deaths are connected, we need to know why one girl was found in Herrington, the other on the moors twenty miles away.'

'So, what do you suggest, David?' asked Bob Harvey.

'We should interview Paul Whittaker again, sir,' said Watkins. 'This time we thoroughly search Janice's bedroom to look for a diary and anything else of interest, and speak to Mrs Whittaker alone. She must be able to help us.'

Cornell answered. 'I agree, but Paul Whittaker has already refused my request to visit his home and search. So, we need a warrant. Sergeant Harvey, get me one. Watkins, after the Whitfield's have identified their daughter, assuming they do, bring them over here for interview, would you? You and Dennison can do it, and where the hell is he, anyway?'

'Not back from the lab yet, sir.'

'Right, I'll go over there myself. I need to speak to the pathologist. Dennison's probably in a separate room recovering from a faint.'

So now we have an aggressive superintendent insisting two cases are not connected when they so very obviously are. And how is he connected to Whittaker? Don't like where this is going. Still no idea who the murderer could be.

CHAPTER EIGHT

Twelve Years ago

It was while Detective Sergeant Max Cornell worked in anti-terrorism that he met a MI5 agent with whom he worked closely, too closely as it happened, for within a short space of time she became pregnant and they moved in together to a rented apartment in Chelsea.

For the following two and a half years the couple enjoyed a happy family life watching their son grow, walking, talking and developing a character.

Marriage was never mentioned, both content with their partner status. They often discussed their dreams of travelling, of owning a home in the country, perhaps somewhere abroad. Both were well paid and although they didn't save, they enjoyed not having to watch every penny. Max Cornell was content.

***

Able to reorganise his day, Max Cornell arrived home early from work one Friday afternoon excited at the prospect of a long overdue weekend away with his family.

He drove into the parking area next to the apartment block, surprised Amy's car was not in its usual spot. Perhaps she had been detained at work. It wouldn't be the first time one of their weekends away had been cancelled.

However, he imagined his partner and son had gone to the shops for some last-minute items. It was just as he started to pack his holdall that he noticed the absence of clothes in the wardrobes.

He found the letter propped against the laptop screen in the small room he and Amy used as an office. The envelope was not sealed and had "Max" written on the front.

The note was short and could just as easily have been from a supplier advising him that the product he had ordered was not in stock. Instead, it said that Amy had gone to America with a returning CIA agent whom she had been seeing for some months. Todd liked him too and they all got on well together.

Max Cornell sat in a chair for the remainder of the day and all of the evening, eventually taking to his bed, fully clothed, in the early hours.

He struggled to come to terms with his loss over the coming days and started drinking excessively, missed work, stopped shaving and neglected the flat as well as himself.

Some nights he just didn't go home. He slept on park benches and in shop doorways. He didn't care anymore.

The helplessness. What was he to do? Go to America and look for his son? Where? And even if he found him, how would he get him home? And how would he look after him once he got him home? No, he decided, Todd was better off where he was. Young enough to forget about his real father.

Why did he think that way?

It was a few months later, at around eleven p.m., that Cornell's superintendent found him arguing with a burly barman as he was being thrown out of a pub in Notting Hill. Cornell was so drunk that the senior police officer was easily able to get him into a taxi and take him to his home, much to his wife's displeasure.

Cornell slept the night in the guest bedroom and was allowed to sleep until late. He awoke to find himself on top of a bed, fully clothed but minus his shoes, with a mouth like the floor of a gorilla's cage and a head like the interior of a joiner's shop.

Wondering where he was, he looked out of the window. There were no familiar high-rise buildings spoiling the view. He could hear birds singing. He was not in his flat, so where the hell was he?

A woman, an apron covering her clothes, came into the bedroom. He didn't recognise her. She carried a small pile of clothes and a cup of coffee, which she placed on the bedside cabinet.

'I am not at all happy that you are in my

home,' she said severely, 'but my husband says you are worth saving. God knows why, and he had better be right. Now, drink your coffee then get a shower because you stink, and put on these clothes. They are my husband's and you and he are about the same size. I'll wash yours.'

She left, shutting the door behind her with a thud.

'Who the hell is she?' he said out loud. 'And where the hell am I?'

He wondered how he was going to get undressed and walk naked in a strange house to find the bathroom, then realised the bedroom had an ensuite. He sat up on the bed and drank the coffee. It tasted awful. He would have much preferred whisky, or brandy maybe.

He would have the shower, but then he would get the hell out of there in his own clothes. Although he was curious as to who thought him worth saving.

Cornell showered but when he returned to the bedroom his own clothes were missing. He dressed in those left for him, finding them a surprisingly good fit. He left the bedroom and walked downstairs towards a room where he could hear a man and a woman talking above the background noise of a washing machine in the room off to his left.

He knocked on the door and entered. The woman who had brought his coffee was sitting on a high stool at a breakfast bar. Sitting beside her was a man Cornell recognised immediately; Detective Superintendent Samuel McNestry.

'Sit and eat,' said the superintendent severely, pointing to both a high stool at the breakfast bar and a rack of toast. 'We assumed you wouldn't want a cooked breakfast.'

Cornell didn't, the thought of it nearly made him sick. He didn't actually want toast either, he'd have much preferred a drink. Beer would do, but he took a slice of toast from the rack and began to spread margarine thinly on it. His head felt queasy, whoever was inside it was currently knocking nails into a hollow object.

There was silence as the man and woman watched him begin to eat the lukewarm toast in small bites.

'How are you feeling?' the woman asked eventually.

'OK, I suppose,' Cornell replied.

'No, you are not,' said McNestry, himself chewing on a loud piece of toast, 'not with the amount of booze you had on board last night, you can't be.'

'Sam, don't be too hard on the boy,' said Mrs McNestry.

'He's not a boy, although he's acting like one.'

Cornell threw down his toast and looked daggers at McNestry who ignored him and continued speaking, and eating. 'You see Margaret, the boy's girl ran off with an American. Took Max's son with her.'

'That's dreadful. But why doesn't Max do something about it?'

'They ran off to America,' her husband replied.

'Oh! I can see his problem,' considered Mrs McNestry.

'And he, instead of manning up, thinks drinking himself to death is the answer,' sounded Sam McNestry.

'How do you know about all this?' demanded Cornell.

'Because you've told everybody who would listen to you.'

'Well, I don't have to listen to you,' said Cornell, rising from his seat.

'Yes, you do. Sit down. I'm not finished with you yet,' bawled McNestry, adding, 'and finish your toast. Now, I'm not going to have you admitted to a rehabilitation clinic, instead, I'm going to arrange for you to be man enough to go cold turkey and return to work on Monday. This period of absence will be put down as sickness.'

'I don't want to go back to work yet,' stated Cornell.

'You don't have a choice.'

'I'll move away.'

'I'll find you.'

'Why are you doing this?' Cornell asked finally.

'Because you are the best damned detective I've ever come across. Better than me and I'm good.'

'You are just sorry for me, that's all.'

'No, I'm not sorry. I actually think your woman slinking off to America with a CIA agent whom she's been seeing behind your back, has some humour attached to it.'

Cornell was outraged. He glared at the senior police officer. The senior police officer glared back at him. Cornell half expected some sympathy from the wife, but she too was glaring at him. She obviously thought his girl leaving him for an American was funny too.

Taking their two-year-old son with her, now being introduced to the American National Football League rather than the English Premier League, speaking in an American accent instead of South London.

The joke, if there was one, was on him. He imagined his work colleagues laughing at his situation. He imagined if he was one of them, he would laugh too. And he did just a little.

'I suppose it is kind of funny,' he said finally.

Superintendent McNestry took Cornell home to his flat, remonstrating with him for its untidiness. McNestry waited until Cornell had changed into clothes of his own, then retrieved his and left, promising to drop the washed clothes off at a later date.

'Good luck Monday, Max,' were his last words.

Max did not reply, but he did return to work on the following Monday.

CHAPTER NINE

Thursday afternoon, present day

Max Cornell had not been to Newcastle's Forensics Laboratories before. He'd been scheduled to visit during his induction on joining the Northumbria force, but something came up and the visit was postponed. The lab and the city morgue were in the same building.

They were not places he enjoyed visiting. Like all the other pathology laboratories he had ever been to, they smelt of what they were. Places of death.

Unsuccessful efforts had been made to brighten this place up by plastering over the highly polished bottle green bricks, but you cannot erase the smell of the death chemicals.

Cornell found DC Dennison looking down through the observation window, completely absorbed in watching Dr Mabel Wainwright at an examination table.

She wore a sleeveless top and trousers covered by a huge grey apron. She wore white trainers on her feet. Around her head was a contraption combining an additional light source and two powerful magnifying lenses.

Mabel Wainwright was poking around the open chest of a male cadaver; her voice describing her discoveries was audible through the speakers in the ceiling.

Dennison, concentrating on the procedure, failed to see Cornell at first, then jumped when he suddenly realised his boss stood alongside him.

'I'm sorry, sir. Got carried away. This is fascinating. We've done the girl found up on the moors, sir, and Doctor Wainwright asked me if I wanted to see this one. I should have come back to the station, I know, and I'm sorry, but I would have been back soon and this is so interesting, sir.'

'It's alright, Ian. I admire your fascination of the dead but this isn't solving our murder, is it?'

'No, sir. Sorry, sir,' Dennison uttered as he moved swiftly to the exit.

'Big, bad boss,' said Mabel Wainwright as the detective constable left them. 'Never known anyone, least of all a copper, so keen to watch an autopsy. I think he's in the wrong job.'

'Who knows what goes through the mind of DC Dennison. He's like the naughty boy that everybody puts up with because of his humour and enthusiasm. However, what, if anything, have you found in whom we believe to be Margaret Whitfield, doctor?'

She ignored him, her attention being with the corpse she was attending.

'Heart attack. Myocardial infarction. That's

the fifth in two days. Almost an epidemic.'

The pathologist washed her hands in a stainless-steel sink. Everything was stainless steel in the morgue.

'I've been so busy, chief inspector. My colleague is off ill and one of my assistants is sunning herself somewhere in the Canaries at this very moment, but I have finished your Margaret.'

'You say that as if there are more girls to find, doctor. Mr and Mrs Whitfield are coming here to identify their daughter later this afternoon, although we are pretty sure this is her. Found anything to help us?'

'Well, I can confirm this young lady was strangled and by someone very strong who used only his left hand to do it.'

'His?'

Wainwright looked up at Cornell.

'That our murderer is a female, chief inspector, is not beyond the bounds of possibility. However, I believe our perpetrator, as well as being strong, must also have been very tall. I estimate six foot six and humans of around that height are generally male.'

'I'll go along with that theory, doctor.'

'And please don't make it public,' she retorted. 'I don't have time to answer hate mail from female wrestlers and basketball players.'

'But why do you think he's six feet six?'

'He would need to be tall to impart the force necessary to strangle someone with just one big hand. Think of the lever principle, chief inspector. That height is my estimate, give or take an inch or two.'

'OK, but why just his left hand?' asked Cornell. 'Surely if you are going to strangle someone, you get both hands to it.'

'Maybe he cannot use his right hand for some reason,' answered the pathologist. 'But you should know, chief inspector, this man is strong, believe me, he's strong. The poor girl's ceratoid arteries, larynx and hyoid bones are completely crushed.'

'Well, that narrows it down a bit,' said Cornell.

'Don't be flippant, chief inspector. Also, this young lady had an abortion about three months ago and I'm waiting for DNA results to see if there was any belonging to someone else on her.'

'Thanks, doctor. Somewhere in all of this there is evidence that leads to a murderer. If only I knew what it was.'

'I can't help you there, chief inspector. Now, I have to return this poor man's organs then have Tom stitch him up.'

Cornell made to leave.

'Are you with somebody, chief inspector? Do you have a wife, a husband, a partner?' the doctor asked with her back to him.

'No, single. Why do you ask?'

'Don't want to step on anyone's toes, but I desperately need an Indian meal and your company during it would be much appreciated.'

The pathologist, not waiting for an answer looked at her watch. 'Meet me in the "Iron Foundry" at eight thirty. We'll go on from there. Mine's a gin and tonic, OK?'

'Is this being recorded, doctor?' asked a surprised and astonished Cornell, spotting the microphones strategically placed in the examination area.'

'Of course.'

'Then I'll see you at eight thirty.'

***

The "Iron Foundry" was a pub across the road from the police station and often frequented by off duty police officers. Cornell arrived at eight fifteen and sitting on a bar stool, ordered himself a pint of John Smith's beer and a gin and tonic for his expected companion.

It had been a while since he had been in female company and he was grateful for that. It was the reason, he told himself, that he had allowed the good doctor to bulldoze him into a dinner date. He didn't consider he was on a date, though. Far from it. He was not the least bit attracted to Doctor Mabel Wainwright, forensic pathologist.

A television with the volume turned down sat behind the bar. It was on the BBC News channel covering the local north east news. Some chap was being interviewed by a reporter who had to stretch her arm holding the microphone to pick up his voice. The text along the bottom of the screen read, Jeremy Symonds MP, Conservative, Berwick upon Tweed.

Must be the guy Lambert was on about. Wearing gloves, not used to North Eastern weather. Wimp.

Cornell wasn't interested in politics. He didn't vote. He had a problem listening to a Labour commentator sounding plausible, then hearing a counter Conservative argument sounding equally plausible.

It was while wondering why all pubs always had their televisions switched on but their volumes turned down, that a female voice spoke from behind him. He turned on his stool and nearly fell off it.

It was true he was not attracted to the forensics pathologist, Dr Mabel Wainwright, but the Ms Mabel Wainwright standing in front of him now had made a physical conversion.

With her fair hair released from a severe pony tail allowing glimpses of gold earrings and her face prettied with makeup, he wanted to say she was beautiful, but he felt that was too audacious. Instead, he said she looked good then realised immediately what a pathetic comment it was.

'May I?' he asked, assisting her to climb on to a bar stool. She opened her coat, but left it on her shoulders.

'Thanks. I hope this is mine.'

She grabbed the gin and tonic in front of her and downed it in one go. 'I needed that. Another of these, please,' she shouted at the barman. 'Do you want another?' to Cornell.

'No thanks. I'm OK.'

'Now, we cannot go through this evening calling one another chief inspector and doctor, so how does Max and Mabel sound?'

'Sounds like a Broadway musical, but it's fine with me.'

'I just love your humour, Max. So, you can now tell me how someone from Manchester happens to have a north eastern accent. You can't have picked up Geordie in only three months.'

'My parents are from the North East, Mabel. I was born and lived in Ryton on Tyne until I was twelve. Then the family moved south. My father was an officer in the army, eventually joining a regiment that required his presence nearer his headquarters. He was in the SAS and was killed in some conflict overseas.'

'Oh! I am sorry. Your poor mother.'

'Oh, she got through it OK. I don't think their marriage was that good when he died.'

Mabel Wainwright looked at her watch.

'We'd better go. I have our table booked for nine. Then you can tell me all about yourself.'

Looking for a very tall, very strong, left-handed murderer while hoping to enjoy dinner with a very forthright, yet beautiful woman (who also looks "good").

CHAPTER TEN

Ten years before

Detective Sergeant Max Cornell took the pick- pocket's arm and led him along to the cells.

'You going to take these handcuffs off me?' the thief begged rather pitifully.

'You going to behave?'

The man nodded and Cornell removed the cuffs.

The man immediately kicked off, lashing out at Cornell catching him on the brow and knocking him backwards. The man ran towards the entrance door, which was being held open by a constable to allow another prisoner through.

'Stop him!' yelled Cornell who ran after his escapee. The constable was quick enough to half close the door allowing Cornell to grasp his prisoner by the scruff of the neck. The man continued to struggle until Cornell, now assisted by the other officer, manhandled the culprit to the floor enabling handcuffs to be reapplied.

Re-entering the main police station concourse, Cornell was brushing off his jacket as he appraised the desk sergeant of the prisoner's situation. No, he didn't want assaulting a police officer added to the charge sheet.

A voice from behind him made him turn around and he came face to face with Superintendent Sam McNestry, dressed in plain clothes. It had been two years since the senior officer had dragged a drunken Cornell into a taxi and took him to his home to sober up.

'Doesn't get any easier, does it Max?' said the senior man, smiling.

'Easier, or better, sir?'

'I know what you mean. You finished for the day?'

'Just the paperwork for this arrest, sir. Why do you ask?'

'Meet me in "The Stag" in an hour.'

Cornell went to his desk and computer where he typed up the arrest of his pickpocket whom he had observed taking wallets, watches and bracelets from several unsuspecting commuters boarding a packed train.

He had marvelled at the skill of the man, sometimes not seeing the actual theft himself, but knowing that it had taken place. Problem was, it wasn't the first time he had arrested the young thief.

Detective Sergeant Max Cornell sat down opposite Superintendent Sam McNestry at a corner table in the lounge of "The Stag." Several uniformed and some plain clothes officers stood around the bar: some were playing pool.

'How's work treating you?' asked the superintendent.

'Are you feeding back to my inspector, sir?'

'Not at all, just wanted to know how you were getting on.'

'Seriously?'

'Seriously.'

'Well, today I've been to a burgled home and a burgled pub. No resources to even attempt to catch the burglars. I've cautioned two lads for using foul language in a supermarket, been to a school because somebody thought a pervert was watching the kids playing. Then I arrested a young pickpocket for about the fourth time.'

'OK, OK, I get the picture, Max. Not the best use of your talents if you ask me. What happened with the anti-terror squad?'

'They thought I was a liability, sir. Couldn't have a drunk working with the anti-terror elite. Thanks to you, I hadn't become a full-blown alcoholic, so giving up the drink wasn't such a problem, but my superiors were not persuaded, so, they put me on plain clothes petty crime until I could show I was fully rehabilitated. That was two years ago, sir. It's doing my head in. It's enough to turn a man to drink.'

McNestry smiled at the comment.

'Beats me why the hierarchy are so short sighted, Max. Did you get any support when you returned to work?'

'Have you taken up comedy, sir?'

The superintendent shook his head. Max waited for the reason the two were sitting in a pub in South London. He didn't have to wait long.

'Max, I've been given a special assignment and I'm about to start recruiting. I want you to be my first appointment.'

'What assignment is that, sir?'

'Organised crime. There has been a massive build up here in London, with direct links to Manchester. There are too many underworld murders, too much high value crime and questions are being asked in the House. You interested?'

'Yes, sir, but why me?'

'You are a fine detective, Max, who has only once run away from trouble and the way you came back from it puts you at the top of my list. I want you to run the Manchester end. You will continue to work for the Met, but you will be stationed in the North West with your own team. We can take the mobsters off the streets, Max.'

'Most of them just get community service, sir.'

McNestry laughed.

'A bit of an exaggeration, Max, but it's true their sentences are too short. The new Home Secretary is putting pressure on the judiciary to use the powers they already have to issue longer sentences. If they don't, the government will legislate that they do.'

'Alright, I'm in,' said a smiling Max Cornell.
McNestry offered his hand to shake.
'Welcome, Detective Inspector Cornell.'

CHAPTER ELEVEN

Thursday evening, present day

Seated at their table in an Indian restaurant, drinks ordered and the customary poppadum and chutney combinations placed on the table, Mabel put her menu down.

'I know what I'm going to have, Max. Do you?'

He decided to play along. He would have liked to peruse what appeared to be an extensive menu, but chicken madras, keema pilau rice and a peshwari naan would do fine.

His dinner cohort's directness attracted him. She reminded him of his mother.

'So, Max, you were telling me about your move south.'

Mabel Wainwright finished chewing a mouthful, wiped her mouth on her napkin and took a swig of Cobra beer. She was smiling and waiting for Cornell to answer.

He told her of his joining the Metropolitan police; of meeting and living with an MI5 agent, who out of the blue took their two-year-old son and went to live in America with a CIA agent whom, according to the note she left him, she had been seeing for some time.

Mabel asked if he had he tried to find them.

No, he answered. Missed his son terribly at first, but he didn't think he would be able to get him out of the States even if he could find them. The boy was probably better off where he was, with his mother.

By the time he was halfway through his madras, he had told her how he moved to serious crime working mostly in Manchester. How he married a police officer from the Manchester force and that when he was close to arresting Manchester's chief crime villain, his wife Michelle was shot and killed.

'I'm so sorry. That must have been terrible.'

'It was,' he answered.

'Did you ever find out who killed her?' Mabel Wainwright asked.

'Oh yes. It was the thug we were trying to bring down: John Thomas Ramsey. One of his lieutenants telephoned the night she died to tell me.'

'God!' she exclaimed. 'How did you cope with that?'

'It wasn't easy. I actually sat in my car one night outside Ramsey's mansion on the Wirral deliberating the best way to kill him.'

'You obviously decided there wasn't one.'

'I did think about breaking into his house when he was out and switching his gas on, then waiting until he returned home and telephoning him. When he lifted the receiver it would break the circuit, creating a spark and causing an explosion.'

'I think I saw that in a film once,' she answered. 'You obviously felt you would never get away with it.'

'No, it wasn't that. They don't have gas in that part of the Wirral.'

Mabel spluttered, reached for her napkin to wipe her mouth and was then able to laugh. She laughed out loud, other customers looked across at her, but she ignored them.

'You are so funny,' she said, returning to her meal. 'So, what happened to this crime boss person?'

'He made a mistake. All criminals do eventually. He killed someone without realising he was being filmed. Little did he know, a mother who blamed him for her son's drug addiction and subsequent death, followed him everywhere biding her time. She gave me the video. He got thirty years.'

Before finishing their meals, he was able to glean from her that apart from her medical training, and a spell of two years in America, during which time she had married, given birth and divorced, she had lived her life in the North East of England. Following in her parents' footsteps she had become a doctor, specialising in pathology out of sheer interest.

Her mother had died some ten years before,

and her father was an alcoholic living somewhere in Yorkshire. He was no longer practising, not because of his age, but struck off for ruining a young girl's chances of becoming a mother.

'So, you have come home,' she stated later as they walked to their vehicles.

'I reckon so. I had become something of a celebrity with the press in Manchester, who were starting to follow me around hoping to see some action. My mother came back north when Dad died and she returned to live in Ryton. The police authorities thought I would live longer if I moved out of Greater Manchester so I moved north too, fortunate to get a chief inspector's post. I have a small house in Cullercoats.'

They reached their parked vehicles.

'Max, thank you for a lovely evening. I have really enjoyed your company. I hope we can do it again.'

Before he could agree, she kissed him briefly on the lips and got into her Porsche 911. She reversed out of her space, gave a toot on the horn and drove off. He stood and watched her vehicle exit the carpark with a squeal of tyres, deciding he had actually enjoyed the evening.

He couldn't believe he had told her most of his life story without getting very much of hers.

But, he concluded, the evening had been pleasant and, yes, he would do it again.

CHAPTER TWELVE

Friday

'Sir,' said Sergeant Harvey, 'dropped an ITO into Judge Cornforth's chambers first thing this morning expecting to get a hearing for a warrant this afternoon, but his clerk has just been on the phone. "No way," she said.'

'Give a reason?' asked Cornell.

'It was something like, "if you think Judge Cornforth is going to issue a warrant against an eminent QC without concrete evidence of a serious crime, you are having a laugh," sir.'

'OK, sergeant.' Then turning his attention to his two male constables, 'Dennison, Watkins, how did you get on with the Whitfield's yesterday?'

'They confirmed the body was Margaret, sir, which we knew they would,' answered Dennison, 'and that Margaret and Janice had been good friends since they first started university.'

'When did the Whitfield's last see their daughter?'

'Last Saturday morning, sir.'

'What time did she leave the home?'

'Around eleven in the morning, sir.'

'Did they know where she was going?' Cornell asked.

'No, sir,' replied DC Watkins. 'They asked, but she wouldn't tell them. Said it was none of their business. They say she was flustered, in a hurry to get away. Her father offered to give her a lift, but she refused, insisting on using her own car.'

Watkins looked at his notes. 'A 2016 Seat Ibiza, sir. We've checked with traffic. It hasn't turned up anywhere.'

'Did they know if she kept a diary?'

'Not that they are aware of, sir, but she could have done as she was always writing when she was younger. She used to write letters to her mother, that sort of thing.'

'OK, Watkins. You and Dennison have a ride out to their home and see if you can find a diary.'

'Yes, sir,' they replied in unison.

'Oh! Did they mention that Margaret had had an abortion about three months ago?'

'No, sir,' said Watkins, 'but it's not something you would disclose without being prompted, is it, sir?'

'That's true, so talk to them about it when you see them,' said Cornell, who then turned back to his second in command. 'Bob, if Janice Whittaker kept a diary, I need it. I also need to speak to Mrs Whittaker. If you can't get Judge Cornforth to give you a warrant, use your charm and get him to see me later today, or first thing tomorrow morning. Tell him it's a matter of extreme importance if he hesitates.'

'Life and death, sir?'

'More important than that.'

***

'Phone call, line two, chief inspector. It's forensics,' called out a young female administrator from a desk thirty feet away.

Cornell picked up a receiver and punched the second digit.

'DCI Cornell.'

'We never exchanged mobile numbers,' said Doctor Mabel Wainwright.

'No, we didn't and perhaps we should have done.'

'Perhaps the next time. I've just got the lab results back for the foreign DNA I found on Margaret Whitfield.'

'Does it tell us anything?'

'Sorry, I ran it through the database and there is no match with anyone.'

'Damn,' exclaimed Cornell.

'But...,' teased Wainwright.

'But what, doctor,' Cornell said impatiently.

'My technical people have been able to enhance a photograph of the strangulation marks around Margaret's neck, which we could compare against a perpetrator if and when we find one.'

'Right. Thanks, doctor. Will be in touch.'

'I hope so,' she said breaking the connection.

Cornell added the new information to the whiteboard then read through everything written on it for the umpteenth time. He was concerned. The information they had on the two deaths still led them nowhere.

***

Lunch time came and went. Cornell's telephone rang.

'Call from the coroner's office, sir,' said the voice putting the call through.

'DCI Cornell,' he said.

'Matthew Dupont, assistant coroner here, chief inspector. Where are we with the investigation into the death of Janice Whittaker?'

'We are not,' answered Cornell. 'Quite sure she drowned, but not sure whether she did it voluntarily. Investigation continuing.'

'It's just that her father, a Mr Paul Whittaker, is getting quite aggressive in wanting her body released, threatening all sorts of legal actions.'

'Are you open minded, Mr Dupont?'

'Yes, I think so; I would like to think so. Why do you ask?'

'Tell Mr Whittaker to piss off.'

'Oh! Right, well, err... yes, I see, yes, right, err... good day, chief inspector.'

***

'Sir!' shouted Sergeant Bob Harvey from his desk. 'Judge Cornforth will see you in his chambers today at four thirty.'

'Tell him I'll be there.'

'He knows that, sir, as he's making a special effort just for you. It would be in the force's best interest if you didn't get lost on the way, sir.'

***

'Support Newcastle United, I hope?' demanded Judge Cornforth who sat behind a huge desk, empty except for Harvey's ITO form requesting a search warrant, in front of him.

Cornell quickly realised that if he said he didn't support Newcastle, his chances of securing a warrant would diminish.

'Very definitely, judge,' Cornell half lied, 'even though I've only been in the North East for three months and ....'

'I've been a season ticket holder for forty-five years,' interrupted the judge, gesturing towards the chair on Cornell's side of the desk. He continued in full flow as Cornell sat down. 'I've watched them through the bad times, which have far outweighed the good times, but this is the worst time I can ever remember. We've had countless managers over the years, mostly bad, but this manager they've got now, he's about as useful as a chocolate fireguard. He's absolutely totally clueless and just has to go.'

'But he's only been at Newcastle since the beginning of this season, judge.'

'Yes, and look where we are! Second off

bottom! And we are only there because we managed to beat the bottom team through a very dubious penalty. We have a defence that has more holes in it than my golf course. A midfield that's about as creative as an episode of Crossroads and strikers that have lost their sense of direction. Anyway, why do you want to invade the home of Paul Whittaker QC?'

Cornell explained the discovery of both girls' bodies, the first visit to Whittaker's home and the man's hostility and non-co-operation, and that Cornell believed there was more to the deaths than meets the eye. He needed to know if Janice Whittaker kept a diary, or held any information in her bedroom that would help the investigation. He also wanted to interview Mrs Whittaker, which Mr Whittaker had objected to.

'How old are you, chief inspector?' asked the judge.

'Forty-two, judge. Why do you ask?' replied Cornell, not understanding the question, or the reason behind it.

'You look younger. You appreciate that Paul Whittaker will raise holy hell if I issue a warrant and you don't find anything. I will lose so much face at the bar that I will be back touting for briefs amongst the legal aid lawyers.'

'Yes, judge.'

'And you don't care, do you?' stated the judge.

'No, judge.'

The judge stared at Cornell for what seemed a long time.

'I've met people like you before, chief inspector, and they weren't chief inspectors.'

'Don't know what you mean, judge.'

'Yes, you do. Usually, it's people who have been through tragedy themselves, maybe more than once. I can see it in your eyes. You've been there and now authority doesn't scare you anymore. If it did, you wouldn't be here requesting a warrant to search an eminent QC's house with no more justification than a gut feeling.'

Cornell sat quiet. There was nothing more he could say to this judge, whom, he decided, was not someone to mess with. This was someone who could switch the conversion in an instant and accurately evaluate the person sitting opposite him in seconds.

The judge expressed a huge sigh. 'However, I confess I too am curious as to why an in demand successful barrister has dropped out of circulation. No doubt I will find out in due course.'

He took out a pocket watch, glanced at it then replaced it in his waistcoat pocket.

'Wait here. I'll see if I have any staff left. They tend to get a flyer on Fridays.'

The judge left the room leaving Cornell by himself. Scanning the room, Cornell could see several certificates and photographs which he would have liked to have perused, but he didn't dare move feeling the judge would know.

The judge soon returned and handed over a signed search warrant.

'Thank you, Judge Cornforth.'

'You are welcome. I hope you find what you are looking for, for my sake. Oh! And good luck with Mrs Whittaker.'

'Why is that, judge?'

'You will be lucky to find her sober.'

No further forward in finding a very strong, left-handed murderer. Not even a suspect.

CHAPTER THIRTEEN

Eighteen months earlier

Police Sergeant Michelle Cornell had rung her husband earlier in the day to say that due to an operational emergency she would not be home until nine in the evening. They had planned to go out for a meal but because of his wife's late availability Max decided he would treat her to a Chinese takeout instead.

He parked his vehicle outside the restaurant at eight fifteen and joined a queue of six waiting to order their takeout's. On the wall behind the serving bar was a television playing Coronation Street, which the Chinese waiter watched avidly when not being interrupted by customers.

As Cornell was giving his order the programme's exit music finished abruptly, then rather than showing an advert the announcer stated that a news bulletin would follow from the Granada news desk. The waiter was about to turn the sound down but at Cornell's barked instruction, left it where it was.

'At six pm this evening,' the newscaster detailed, 'there was a shooting in the Moss

Side area of Manchester where Granada TV has been informed, a police officer has been fatally wounded. We understand that the officer is a sergeant and female. The reason behind the exchange of gun fire between police and what we believe to be gang members is not known at this stage. Names are not being released until relatives have been informed.'

Cornell acquired his Chinese meals and headed for home. He had thought of cancelling the order as he knew the meals would never be eaten.

He arrived home at ten minutes after nine and knew Michelle would not be there. He knew Michelle would never be coming home as he knew Michelle was the female police sergeant referred to in the TV bulletin.

He would never be able to explain how he knew for certain, but he knew. He was experiencing the same empty feeling he had felt after reading the note Amy left for him all those years ago. The feeling of loneliness, of isolation and solitude.

He sat at the breakfast table, the unopened Chinese meals in their carrier bags in front of him.

He placed his mobile phone on the table, although he knew they would not tell him over the phone. He wondered who the officers charged with the task of informing him his wife was dead would be.

He was not on the Greater Manchester Constabulary payroll, but doubted it would be anyone from the Met. Not this soon afterwards.

But it was not a knock on the door or the ring of his mobile that occurred, but the ring of his landline. He arose from the table and went to the hall where the landline telephone, rarely used, was located. He lifted the receiver.

'Hello.'

'Cornell?' asked the voice.

'Who is calling?'

'You seen the news?'

'Yes, but who is this?'

'Just a messenger to tell you that the copper who was killed tonight was your wife. We told you to back off, Cornell. This is what happens when you don't.'

'Fine, you've told me. So, you go and tell your boss, your plan hasn't worked. I'll come after him even more now and I'll catch him soon. I always do and he'd better hope I'm not alone.'

The line went dead.

Cornell came back into the kitchen. Threw the Chinese meals into the waste bin and sat and thought. He tried to make sense of his options for the future, but they just kept tumbling over in his mind. How to catch John Thomas Ramsey and how to live alone became enmeshed.

The loud knock on his door startled him. He opened it to a uniformed male superintendent and female inspector from the Manchester constabulary.

For some reason which he never quite

understood, they always did it this way in Manchester.

A senior male officer for authority and a female officer for sympathy.

Cornell invited the two officers in and offered them seats at the kitchen table.

'I know why you're here,' he said.

The officers looked at each other.

'But we haven't announced any names yet.'

'I saw the bulletin on the news earlier. I suspected it could be Michelle, but I've just had one of John Thomas Ramsey's lieutenants on the phone to confirm it is her.'

'You mean Ramsey's informed you?' exclaimed the female of the two.

'Yes. The messenger said she had died because of my investigation of Ramsey and that I hadn't backed off when advised to.'

'And will you now?' asked the superintendent.

'Not bloody likely,' Cornell said quietly, 'there's a revenge aspect to it now.'

'Max,' said the superintendent, 'I'm here at the bequest of your superintendent, Sam McNestry. He apologises for his absence, but he couldn't be here tonight anyway. He sends his condolences and will come and see you shortly. You are to telephone him if you need anything.'

'Thank you, sir,' said Cornell.

'You seem to be taking it very well, inspector,' said the junior of the two officers.

'I've been through something like this before, inspector. Not a death, more of being left alone after losing both your partner and son. I have developed coping mechanisms.'

After the two officers left Cornell went to bed and cried.

CHAPTER FOURTEEN

Saturday, present day

'Why are all these detectives in on a Saturday, chief inspector?' asked Chief Superintendent Mark Braithwaite.

'Investigating a murder, sir,' replied Cornell, displaying a huge smile.

Braithwaite stood red faced with fury. He wanted to say something about overtime, budgets and costs, but hesitated. The room had gone completely quiet to hear his response to Cornell's sarcasm. He glared at Cornell, struggling and failing to think of an appropriate retort.

'Carry on,' he said storming from the incident room.

The team took to their seats in front of the whiteboard.

'Where are we with tracing Janice's and Margaret's vehicles?' Cornell asked.

'No sign of either of them anywhere, sir.'

'Watkins, the visit to the Whitfield's; I understand they are fairly well off and have a big house?'

'I should say so, sir. Dennison got lost twice.'

The team laughed. Cornell had decided not to discourage humour in meetings. When you are discussing murder and death it is often necessary to lighten the mood.

'So, we have friends, Miss Whittaker and Miss Whitfield, both from posh homes. Both about twenty years of age, both died within two days of each other. And what about a diary?'

'No such luck, sir. We looked all over Margaret's bedroom, even checked for loose floor boards, but couldn't find anything that would be of interest.'

'But all girls keep a diary, don't they? Donaldson, do you keep a diary, or did you at their age?'

'No, sir.'

'Bugger. So, what else if anything, did you discover?'

Dennison answered, reading from his note book. 'Margaret was an only child. Very good at school. Got good 'A' levels. Got into Newcastle University, met Janice Whittaker there and they became friends. Everything alright until about three months ago.'

'What happened three months ago?' asked Cornell.

'Margaret's personality changed,' chipped in Watkins. 'She became bad tempered, disrespectful and offensive, was how Mrs Whitfield put it. She was living-in at university but coming home at weekends. Then she started to come home on a Friday afternoon to drop off and pick up her washing, then she started staying out at weekends too.'

'For what purpose?' asked Cornell.

'She wouldn't say, which was the cause of the rows.'

'What about her pregnancy?' asked Harvey.

'Yes, we asked them about that,' answered Watkins. 'It came as a shock to the parents. She told them during an argument. They wanted to be supportive, but Margaret wouldn't let them. She arranged an abortion herself.'

'Did they have any idea who the father was?'

'No idea, sir, and the parents were not aware of a boyfriend,' said Dennison.

'Did you ask them if they'd ever met Janice?'

'Yes, sir,' replied Watkins. 'She had stopped over a couple of times, but they were not in her company long enough to form an impression, other than she seemed like a nice girl.'

'When was the last time she stopped over?'

'About four months ago, sir. Just before the arguments started,' said Watkins.

The pertinent parts from the interview were added to the whiteboard.

'Did the parents have any idea where Margaret's car may be?' asked Cornell.

'No, sir,' replied Watkins.

'So,' challenged Cornell, 'what could have caused a personality change in Miss Whitfield?'

'Be interesting to know if Janice suffered one

as well,' queried Donaldson. 'She did drop out of university.'

'We might find out in a couple of hours. I have a warrant for Whittaker's. Who is free this afternoon to exercise a search warrant?'

Everyone but Dennison put their hands up.

'Sorry, boss, but I've arranged to go to the match.'

'You have a season ticket?'

'Yes, sir. Both me and wor lass.'

Cornell had always struggled with the "wor lass" Geordie colloquialism, which far from being insulting, was considered endearing when referring to one's wife or girlfriend.

'Apparently Judge Cornforth has a season ticket too,' offered Cornell.

'I know, sir. His seat is next to ours. You should hear him swear, sir, and it's not just bugger and damn.'

Margaret's attitude changed 3 months ago. Janice dropped out of university shortly afterwards. Does that have anything to do with this murder? Still clutching at straws.

CHAPTER FIFTEEN

Saturday afternoon

Cornell gave the warrant to Laura Donaldson to execute as the four police officers lined up at Paul Whittaker's front door. The Beethoven riff created by the doorbell could be heard from inside. The door swung open.

'Mr Paul Whittaker,' said DC Donaldson, 'I have a warrant to search these premises...'

Whittaker snatched the warrant from her.

'Who has issued this?'

Cornell took a pace forward and snatched the warrant back.

'You, sir, will show my officers some respect. As of now, we are in charge here. You know how this works, so keep out of our way,' instructed Cornell, stuffing the warrant inside Whittaker's waistcoat and pushing him back inside the house.

'I'll see about this!' Whittaker said angrily, picking up the telephone receiver from the hallway table and punching out digits with grim determination.

'Right. Donaldson,' said Cornell, 'you see to Mrs Whittaker. Sergeant Harvey, you and Watkins take the bedrooms. I'll just mooch around down here.'

As Cornell mooched, Whittaker could be heard on the hall telephone complaining loudly and bitterly to someone. Whoever it was Cornell couldn't imagine, but the conversation didn't last long. Whittaker slammed the receiver down and stormed into the lounge.

'You are not to go upstairs!' he yelled at the three officers as they disappeared up the spiral stairway. 'How dare you! I will have your jobs for this!'

Whittaker ran upstairs after them, only to be confronted by Harvey who threatened to handcuff him if he didn't allow the warrant to be executed in accordance with the law. Cornell thought he should assist.

As he arrived on the landing, Donaldson appeared from a bedroom.

'Sir, I think you had better see this.'

Cornell noticed there was a key in the lock on the outside of the door. Venturing in to the bedroom, which stank of stale alcohol, he saw a semi-conscious and half-dressed Joan Whittaker slumped in a chair by an unmade bed. The woman's eyes focused on Cornell, just about.

'Thank God,' she muttered. 'Please help me.'

Harvey and Watkins continued to restrain an enraged Whittaker outside the bedroom.

'Don't say anything, Joan!' shouted Whittaker from the landing. 'You know I always look after you!'

Cornell knelt on one knee in front of Joan Whittaker and took her hands.

'How would you like us to help you, Mrs Whittaker?'

'I need help. I'm in jail. Get me out of jail.'

'Don't listen to her! She's not well,' shouted Whittaker, who was being manhandled downstairs.

'Would you like us to take you to hospital, Mrs Whittaker?'

'Oh! Yes, please. That would be nice. Thank you,' she said, nodding her head and appearing very grateful for that suggestion.

'Laura, call an ambulance, would you? I'll leave you with her. Help her get dressed and see if you can get her downstairs.'

Cornell went back downstairs to allow his two officers to search the bedrooms. Whittaker now had his hands cuffed behind him and was sitting uncomfortably on the long leather sofa.

'Unlawful search,' he said. 'I'll have this before a judge in no time. How dare you restrain me. Do you know who I am?'

'Mr Whittaker, we are calling an ambulance as we don't think Mrs Whittaker is very well.'

'She's just a bit under the weather that's all. You have no right to undermine my authority. She'll be alright in a couple of days.'

Sergeant Harvey entered the lounge.

'Sir, there are four bedrooms, two of them

obviously girls' bedrooms, but one doesn't appear to have been slept in ever. The other, we think was Janice's bedroom because we found a letter addressed to her. Watkins found a couple of diaries in an overhead cupboard, last year's and this. The diaries are locked, sir, but shouldn't be a problem to open. In what we think is the main bedroom, we found this.'

Watkins held a laptop.

'You have no right to take that!' yelled Whittaker. 'It's private and personal. Your warrant doesn't cover the removal of items.'

'I think, Mr Whittaker, you will find that it does. But tell me, sir, why do you lock your wife up in her bedroom?'

'You can go to hell,' was the response.

'Been there, done it, Mr Whittaker.'

Meanwhile, Laura Donaldson had helped Joan Whittaker down the stairs.

'I'm so sorry. So embarrassed,' she said weeping.

'That's alright, Mrs Whittaker. We will get you some help.'

'Thank you, thank you. He did this to me, the bastard,' she said, glaring at her husband.

'Don't talk now,' said Cornell. 'We will speak to you when you are a little better.'

An ambulance siren could be heard in the distance.

'That will be for us,' said Donaldson.

'That was quick. Eighteen minutes,' Cornell

said after looking at his watch.

While the paramedics were assisting Joan Whittaker into the ambulance, Bob Harvey entered the lounge and confronted Whittaker.

'There's a 2016 Seat Ibiza in your garage, Mr Whittaker. Does it belong to you?'

'Go to hell,' Whittaker replied.

'Mr Whittaker,' Harvey continued, 'we believe that vehicle belonged to a Margaret Whitfield who was murdered a few days ago.'

Whittaker just stared at Harvey; his face impassive.

'Mr Whittaker, can you tell us how the car got to be in your garage?'

No answer.

'Caution him, Bob, and we'll take him in for questioning,' said Cornell.

'One phone call?' asked Whittaker.

'Make it,' replied Cornell.

We now have diaries and a car belonging to a murdered girl; found in the garage of the father whose daughter, the murdered girl's friend, was also found dead. Moving forward, but it's getting complicated.

CHAPTER SIXTEEN

Saturday evening

You've done what!' screamed Mark Braithwaite down the telephone line at Chief Inspector Max Cornell, who was only informing his boss out of courtesy. He would think twice about doing it again.

'Arrested Paul Whittaker, sir. He's got a dead girl's car in his garage.'

'That doesn't mean he's a murderer.'

'Never said he was, sir.'

'For God's sake! Don't you know who he is? He's a bloody QC, of all things.'

'Oh! That's all right then. Do you want me to let him go and not bother about the car? That'll go down a bomb with the press. Will you announce it, or shall I?' but Chief Superintendent Braithwaite had already rung off before Cornell could finish his question.

***

'Sir,' said Sergeant Harvey to Cornell, 'Whittaker's solicitor is demanding his client either be charged with a crime or released immediately.'

'Who is his solicitor?'

'The Honourable Lord Sir Anthony Bedwell-Sloan, sir.'

'He the Lord Bedwell-Sloan that sits in the House of Lords and was always on current affairs programmes?'

'The very same, sir, although not often nowadays. One of the last of the hereditary peers. He lives in a hall up near Hexham. His legal practice in Newcastle is Marshall Franks and Bedwell-Sloan. Specialises in church affairs and defending the rich.'

'Has he had enough time with his client?'

'About half an hour, sir.'

'That's long enough. Let's get this interview underway. I think you and I should do this one, OK?'

'Yes, sir,' agreed Harvey.

'Sir,' called Watkins from his desk.

'What?' Cornell responded.

'Managed to get into Janice's diaries.'

'Anything?'

'Not much, sir. There are appointments like dentist, hairdresser and university stuff like lectures, places she visited, then there's a load of capital letters that don't make any sense, sir.'

'Leave it for now. Come in tomorrow, then you and Ian can have a go working out what the capital letters mean.'

***

'Time 20.37, Saturday 19th January 2019. Present: Paul Whittaker, his solicitor, Sir Anthony Bedwell-Sloan, Detective Chief Inspector Max Cornell and Detective Sergeant Robert Harvey.'

'Mr Whittaker, please state your full name for the tape,' commanded Harvey.

'Paul Silas Warrington Whittaker, QC,' Whittaker rasped, emphasising the QC.

'Now that we have the preliminaries out of the way, chief inspector, on behalf of my client I would like to....'

'Mr Bedwell-Sloan, you are not conducting this interview. I am,' said Cornell sternly.

'You will address me with my full name and correct title, sir,' the titled solicitor responded.

Cornell ignored him.

'Mr Whittaker, will you tell us why you have a car registered to a Margaret Whitfield in your garage?'

'No comment.'

Cornell asked him again and received the same answer.

'Is this going to be a one way "no comment" interview?'

'No comment,' replied Whittaker with a wide smirk.

It was then Cornell suddenly realised he had made a blunder.

If Whittaker keeps his mouth shut, there is

nothing to charge him with. So, he had a car in his garage belonging to a girl who had been murdered. Any decent first year articled clerk could argue their way out of that.

'OK, interview terminated 20.42,' said Cornell.

'Is that it, chief inspector?' cried Bedwell-Sloan.

'Unless your client is going to afford us with judicious answers, there doesn't seem much point in continuing at this time,' responded Cornell.

Whittaker leant forward over the table towards the two policemen.

'If you check my record, chief inspector, you'll find I'm a QC who wins many more cases than he loses.'

Cornell leant forward across the table forcing Whittaker backwards.

'And if you check my record, Mr Whittaker, you will find that most of my arrests end up in court with the culprit being found guilty, so, you had better hope I don't arrest you. And, Mr Whittaker, I've taken down far bigger folk than common or garden barristers.'

'That's enough for now,' interrupted Bedwell-Sloan. 'Paul, keep your mouth shut.'

Turning to Cornell, 'Unless you are going to charge my client, chief inspector, I think we are done here. There is a rational explanation for this vehicle being in Mr Whittaker's garage, which we will divulge on condition my client is not rearrested, or brought in for further questioning.'

Bedwell-Sloan knew Cornell would not agree to that, which is why he said he would divulge the "rational explanation," when there may not be one.

'No comment,' answered Cornell, who walked and stood at the door, holding it open for the solicitor and his client to leave. 'You are free to go.'

'Bit of a waste of time, sir,' said Bob Harvey after Whittaker and his solicitor had left.

'I should have thought it through, Bob. I let Whittaker's arrogance get to me. Of course we know it's highly irregular for Whittaker to have a car belonging to a murdered girl in his garage, but I suddenly realised we had nothing to hold him on. The car could have been there since Saturday. Margaret could have driven it there herself.'

Cornell also knew that holding Paul Whittaker any longer could compromise the murder enquiry, although until he connected all the dots, he wasn't sure how.

He and Harvey returned to the incident room to find Laura Donaldson was still working.

'Laura, you should have gone home by now. But be here first thing tomorrow. You too, Bob.'

The two dead girls were involved in something. But what? Whittaker could also be involved. Dead girl's car in his garage, hostile attitude, suspicious reaction to his daughter's death. Along with

Braithwaite, too hasty to hide the cause of her death as suicide. Are Braithwaite and Whittaker linked with something? If so, what? Does it involve the two dead girls? What, if anything, do the capital letters in Janice's diaries mean? This is straying from finding the murderer! But it surely is connected.

CHAPTER SEVENTEEN

Sunday

With the exception of Laura Donaldson, the rest of the team looked as if they had had a few drinks the previous evening. On the bright side, there was no Braithwaite present today to complain about overtime.

'Morning, everyone!' shouted Cornell, louder than he needed to. The three men sitting in front of the whiteboard flinched painfully and groaned. Cornell sat on the corner of an adjacent desk. 'Let's do a recap. You start, Laura.'

'Janice Whittaker, found dead one week ago today, Herrington Harbour, drowned. No evidence on her body to suggest murder. Margaret Whitfield, friend, found dead three days later near Rothbury, murdered.'

'Strangled by a powerful male who used only one hand to do it; his left,' interjected Bob Harvey.

'We don't know how Miss Whittaker got to Herrington, where she went when she got there, or what she was doing while she was there,' added Dennison.

'However, Margaret Whitfield's car turns up in Paul Whittaker's garage,' said Watkins. 'We don't know how it got there either, and Whittaker isn't telling us.'

'Any sign yet of Janice's Citroen anywhere in Tyne and Wear, Northumberland or County Durham?' queried Cornell.

'No, sir,' responded Bob Harvey. 'It could be parked up, but not in Herrington. If it's on the move, I suspect it will have false plates, but according to Traffic, no ANPR has been tripped.'

'Right, I've spoken to their inspector to have them stop all blue Citroen C3's spotted in the North East, but they haven't seen one yet,' stated Cornell.

'What about Whittaker's laptop?' asked Harvey.

'From what we could see, sarge,' said Watkins, 'there were only Word files regarding old clients and what appeared to be legit email correspondence. I have passed it over to IT, but they don't work weekends.'

'OK, chase it up tomorrow. Anything else, sir?' asked Harvey.

'Has Margaret's car been brought in yet, Bob?'

'Yes, sir. Forensics will start on it tomorrow.'

'Right, Laura, in the meantime, go and see Joan Whittaker in hospital. Find out if she knew what was going on with her daughter. Then go home and enjoy the rest of your Sunday.'

***

Max Cornell sat, one leg across the other and hands behind his head scrutinising the whiteboard. He seemed to find some comfort in doing so. Harvey and Dennison joined him.

It was Harvey who spoke first, turning to his subordinate.

'Ian, have you and Watkins found anything in Janice's diaries?'

'Err, no, sarge. I asked Laura to have a look to see if there is like, err…, what girls would, err… sort of put, sir. You know what I mean?' The embarrassed officer continued. 'She couldn't, err…, see anything either. David and I think the pairs of capital letters could be shorthand, either referring to some kind of event, or the initials of people. They started appearing about six months ago.'

Cornell was about to return to his office, but stopped and turned back to Dennison.

'Were there any pairs of letters for the Saturday she died, Ian?'

'Just a second.'

Ian Dennison flicked through the diary pages. 'Yes, sir. There was one pair for the Saturday night and two pairs on the Sunday. One of Sunday's entries is the same as the Saturday's entry.'

Dennison offered the pages in the diary for Cornell to view. The Saturday and Sunday entries meant nothing to him.

'OK, give me a list of all the capital letters, Ian. If they are initials, I don't suppose any of them mean anything?'

'No, sir. Not a thing.'

Cornell returned to his office. He knew he should spend more time in it, but he'd much rather be out in the incident room with his detectives, solving crime. It seemed the higher up the ladder in police echelons you go, the more paperwork there was to do and if you didn't attend to it, it built up exponentially.

He retrieved a folder from the top of his bulging in tray.

Some remote government department requesting the numbers of ethnic minority police officers in his team. He crumpled the request and dropped it in the waste paper basket.

The next folder included an invitation from Human Resources to nominate officers for diversity training. That joined the first request.

He didn't bother looking at any more folders.

Instead, he fired up his laptop and loaded the case file database. He was curious to know more about the notorious William "Buffalo Bill" Tierney case that caused Paul Whittaker to take a break from his profession.

The case notes reminded him of the crime scene in Manchester, but on a much smaller scale.

According to the file, Tierney was a racketeer who came through the ranks of criminal soldiery to become the crime boss on Tyneside. He'd been around on the one-armed bandit scene of the sixties and seventies, graduating to drugs and prostitution in the eighties, protection and people trafficking in the nineties with much else in between. According to his date of birth, he was now seventy-three.

Cornell read on. Many serious assaults and a couple of murders had been attributed to Tierney's organisation. It was the latest of the two murders, a shooting inside one of his night clubs, that had seen him arrested.

Witnesses had made statements placing Tierney in the club on the night of the murder and had observed the argument at the roulette table, the time it occurred, who Tierney was with, and when he and the murdered man left the club together.

Turning his attention to the forensics, the weapon used was a Smith and Wesson .38 revolver. Tierney's fingerprints were the only ones on the gun.

After studying the file Cornell was confused. There was no way the prosecution should have lost this case. According to the notes there were both evidence and witnesses, so what the hell went on in court?

He searched for and found the court case records. It appeared that the witnesses who could be found had changed their statements and may not have seen Tierney and the victim together.

All witnesses were suddenly vague about their movements on the night in question.

There was something wrong here. What happened in court didn't match with what was in the case notes. How could that be?

***

The constant ringing of a telephone in the incident room was annoying him. He looked out of his window and saw both Dennison and Harvey on the phone, Watkins was nowhere in sight. He picked up his receiver and collected the call.

'DCI Cornell.'

'Oh! That was lucky. Am I interfering with anything?' asked Doctor Mabel Wainwright.

'Not exactly,' replied Cornell. 'Didn't know you worked Sunday's, doctor.'

'Catching up, but I will have all my staff back tomorrow. How's your case going?' the doctor asked.

'It isn't.'

'Good, then what you need is a Chinese. I'll meet you in the "Iron Foundry" at half past seven, OK?'

'OK, but can you make it eight o'clock, because I'm recording an appeal for information for the TV at six.'

'Oh! I thought your superintendent didn't like the press.'

'He doesn't, but he's not in today. I'm in charge.'

'Oooooooh, I just love your dominance,' replied Mabel Wainwright as she ended the call.

***

Just before he left the station for his dinner date, the news agency people having left, Laura Donaldson rang in.

'What you got, Laura?'

'I'm afraid Mrs Whittaker is not going to be any help to us, sir.'

'Oh? How's that?' asked Cornell.

'She's going up the wall needing a drink. Pink elephant's upside down on the ceiling and giant blue and yellow striped snakes in her bed, that sort of thing. A nurse said it's called the DT's.'

'Yeah, delirium tremens. It's one of the effects of alcohol withdrawal,' described Cornell, appreciating that he had not suffered with them himself when he had stopped drinking to excess.

'Also, she keeps pulling out the drips and tubes and they have had to restrain her with straps to stop her from endangering herself. The ward sister told me she was going to be moved to another hospital more capable of treating her.'

'That's a shame. But she will come out the other side, won't she? I had hoped she could have thrown some light on what her daughter was up to.'

'Sir, my prognosis for what it's worth, is that Joan Whittaker will not be seeing the light of day for some time, if ever again. I think she has gone quite mad, sir.'

'OK, Doctor Donaldson, that'll do for today. See you in the morning.'

Seems that whatever Whittaker and Braithwaite are involved in, came after the Tierney trial. What happened? A weird murder case. What to do next?

CHAPTER EIGHTEEN

Monday

Max Cornell turned over in bed. He glanced at his watch. Seven a.m. and still dark. The curtains were open, but the outside lights were coming from different angles this morning. This was hardly surprising because he was not in his own bed.

Mabel Wainwright stood silhouetted in the bedroom doorway watching him. From the landing light behind her, he could see she was attired in a thin green dressing gown and didn't appear to have anything on underneath it. She held a coffee. Cornell pulled himself further up on to the pillow and stared back at her for a moment.

'Any chance of a coffee?' he asked.

Mabel Wainwright about turned and walked off downstairs, returning moments later and handed him a coffee in a mug with "Best Mam" printed on it. He looked at it with curiosity then took it from her as she sat down beside him on the bed.

They had not spoken about work the previous evening. Instead, they talked of each other's childhoods and early lives; their likes, dislikes, and achievements away from work. They laughed a lot.

She told him she had a daughter, currently on vacation with her father in America. Cornell wondered about that. Had the daughter remained in England, she would only have been on holiday.

He did not question the break up with her husband, nor did he talk about his son.

'So, what's on the agenda for you today?' she enquired.

'I'm hoping for a break in these cases.'

'Or case. I thought the two dead girls were connected.'

'I'm sure they are, but we are still no further forward in discovering why one may have taken her own life, and who murdered the other.'

'Max, has it occurred to you that the two girls may have been prostitutes?'

'Yes, it has, Mabel; the fact both of them stopped out at weekends and no one knows what they got up to. But I have nothing to back it up. Why do you think it?'

'Just my inquisitive mind working overtime. A serious gut feeling if you like, and it would fit. Both girls, but on different occasions, meeting the same client who was big and strong. Someone who was rough with them and they didn't like it. One girl escaped, but met her death anyway. The other didn't, so he killed her.'

'That sounds very feasible, but...'

'But, I have nothing forensically to back it up either.'

'And if Paul Whittaker QC is involved, why would he condone his daughter being subjected to that?'

'You will have to think out of the box, Max,' said Mabel Wainwright, adding 'and you need to be properly prepared for the day.'

Mabel Wainwright took Cornell's coffee from him and placed it with her own on the dresser, threw off her dressing gown and climbed back under the duvet.

***

Appeals for information on local radio and television always generated hundreds of calls from the public. There were those who had credible information, those who thought they had, and others who rang in just for the hell of it.

Cornell stood with a coffee in hand in the middle of the fray, listening to his officers and others drafted in for the purpose, talking to callers.

'Call for you, sir,' said a young female draftee officer. He took the phone receiver from her.

'DCI Cornell,' he answered.

'PC Dennis Hargreaves here, sir. Remember me from Herrington, the day the young lass was found in the harbour?'

'Yes, Dennis, of course I remember you. You know everyone in Herrington.'

"I thought I did, until that poor girl turned

up dead. Sir, I came across something last night, that kept both me and the missus awake and I think you should know about it.'

'Oh, and what's that?'

Cornell braced himself for the answer, dismissing the vision conjured up by Hargreaves declaration.

'Well, me and Maureen, that's my wife, went for an Indian in Herrington last night. Now, directly opposite the restaurant and next to the Co-op, is a craft shop, you know, one of those that sells wool, cottons, threads, that sort of thing.'

'I think so,' Cornell responded.

'Well, me and Maureen were in the Indian for about two hours. It was our wedding anniversary, you see, been married eighteen years. Anyway, it was pretty busy as it always is on a Sunday night.'

'Right, and happy anniversary,' Cornell said, impatiently wondering where this conversation was going and more importantly, when.

'Thank you, chief inspector. Sir, this may be nothing, but between the hours of twenty thirty and twenty-two thirty, four people entered the craft shop at different times. They were dropped off at the door in posh vehicles, one a Bentley. I thought that was strange, sir.'

'I'm inclined to agree, Dennis. Why were four people visiting a craft shop after eight o'clock on a Sunday night?'

'Exactly, sir, and I can tell you one visitor

was a well-known rock guitarist called Stuart Turner. Me and Maureen are into heavy metal, sir. And another I recognised was a prominent television quiz show host, Simon Kane. I didn't recognise the other two; one was a black guy wearing a white suit. Chief inspector, my Maureen thinks upstairs above the craft shop is a knocking shop, sir.'

'And your Maureen could well be right, Dennis. If she is, do you think the dead girl we found floating face down in the harbour last Sunday morning could possibly have run from this craft shop last Saturday night?'

'It never entered my head that the wee lass was a call-girl, sir, but it is possible she came from there. My Maureen thinks definitely so. At the moment, sir, I'm standing opposite the shop. Maureen went in to buy something on a pretence and says it is a bone fide craft shop, and she would know. She says there is a door through to the back, but there would be, wouldn't there? There was no noise coming from upstairs and looking at it from across the road, sir, I think the upstairs extends to above the house next door.'

Cornell asked Hargreaves for the address.

'Dennis, you obviously think this shop and whatever, if anything, goes on upstairs is worth investigating.'

'I do, sir.'

'So do I, Dennis. However, I want to hold off for the minute. I think there is something big going on and the two dead girls were involved. I would like to find out what that was before risking compromising a murder enquiry.'

'I understand, sir. Chief inspector, is there a sex ring operating on my patch?'

'Possibly, Dennis. At least some of it on your patch. Keep an eye on the place for me, would you?'

'You can bet your bottom dollar on that, sir.'

***

'Sergeant Harvey,' Cornell shouted above the noise of phone call conversations.

'Here, sir,' a voice answered from across the room.

'Sergeant,' said Cornell walking to Harvey's desk and handing him a sheet of paper, 'find out who owns this shop in Herrington, would you? and whether the upstairs is owned by the same person. If not, who owns it? PC Hargreaves' missus suspects it is a brothel and I'm inclined to agree. It may be where Janice Whittaker was and ran from last Saturday night.'

'Chief Inspector,' called another draftee officer, 'I have a young lady on the phone who says she has some information about Janice Whittaker, but she will only speak to you. Won't give her name. Line three.'

Cornell got to a phone, lifted the receiver and pressed digit three.

'Hi, I'm Max Cornell. How can I help you?'

'Are you the policeman who was on the

television last night?'

'Yes, that was me. Do you have any information that can help us?'

'Can't speak over the phone. Can we meet?'

'Certainly. Where and when?'

There was a long pause. Cornell thought she had rung off. His heart was pumping.

'Leazes Park, first entrance on Richardson Road. I'll be on the left side as you enter in half an hour. Come alone.'

The call ended abruptly.

***

Detective Chief Inspector Cornell entered Leazes Park within twenty-five minutes of the call. He had never been to the park before and was faced with several pathways. St. James Park football ground stood towering in the distance. There was no one in sight.

'Damn,' he said out loud, deciding the call must have been hoax. It hadn't sounded hoax, but then hoaxers are not going to sound like hoaxers. He turned towards some trees and a young woman, late teens he would guess, came out from behind one.

'Cornell?' she asked.

'I am.'

She walked off the grass on to the concrete path and looked right and left, then behind her. Being January, there were few people in the park. It had stopped snowing but it was bitterly cold, despite the clear blue sky. The young woman walked up to him. She wore black jeans, a blue jacket, too light for the weather Cornell thought, a pompom hat and well-worn mittens.

'Let's walk,' she said and to his surprise she linked his arm. They walked half a dozen paces before Cornell spoke.

'You rang me,' he said finally. 'You said you had some information on Janice Whittaker, but first of all, what's your name?'

'My name is Sadie. I'm a student at Newcastle University. I knew both Janice and Margaret Whitfield.'

'What can you tell me about them?'

'You have to realise, Mr Cornell, we are watched like hawks and if I'm seen talking to the police I could end up like Margaret.'

'You know about Margaret?'

'I know she's dead,' Sadie answered.

'Did Margaret talk to the police?'

'She tried to.'

'What about Janice?'

'She was causing problems for everyone.'

'Tell me about it, Sadie.'

'There were six of us students who joined in the last six months and another dozen or so girls who had been around for a while. I only know some of their first names. We all work for the club.'

Sadie looked around for the third time. She still linked Cornell's arm and he could feel the tension in her. He knew if he pushed her, she would clam up.

'What club?' he asked, trying to make sense of what she was saying.

'It's a sort of a…. Oh shit!' she exclaimed suddenly. 'I have to go.' She released his arm and sprinted off towards the park entrance.

'Sadie, wait!' he shouted, but she was not going to stop and fit as he was he was not going to catch her.

Cornell looked around to see what had frightened her. He spotted a man wearing dark glasses and speaking into a mobile phone on a pathway that led through the trees. The man turned and walked out of view. Cornell followed him and came to a lake, but the man must have taken a different path as he was nowhere in sight.

**

'All I've got is her first name; Sadie, and that she was a student. That's not a common first name. Donaldson, get on to the university and check it out.'

Cornell was furious with himself. He knew the girl had information crucial to the case and he had let her slip away. He could have asked her about the craft shop in Herrington and about Janice's father. Whether Margaret had a boyfriend. If not, who was the father of her lost child? Damn.

Harvey, Dennison and Watkins stood around him as he told them what Sadie had said.

'There were more than a dozen or so girls,

six were students who had joined this club in the last six months. Sadie said that they were being watched all of the time. I can vouch for that.'

Cornell explained there had been a man in the park whose presence had frightened Sadie, but he disappeared amongst the trees.

***

Learning that the calls made as a result of the news bulletin had, with the exception of Sadie, produced absolutely nothing. Cornell retired to his office. The list of initials from Janice's diary for the Saturday night he had requested from Dennison were on his desk. None of them meant anything to him.

Cornell put his feet on his desk, leant back in his chair and reflected. He now believed Mabel Wainwright was right. Janice Whittaker was a sex worker and they had found where she probably ran from on the Saturday night of her death.

'Come in,' Cornell commanded at a knock on his door.

'Two Sadie's at the university, sir,' said Laura Donaldson. 'A Sadie Hawkshaw from Cumbria, she is days away from becoming twenty-one years of age, studying physics, and a Sadie Tomkinson from Bensham, Gateshead, studying philosophy. Aged nineteen, almost twenty.'

'Check 'em out, Laura, would you?'

'I have, sir. Sadie from Cumbria spoke to her parents last night about her upcoming birthday party. Doesn't sound like your Sadie, sir. On the other hand, Sadie from Gateshead left home two months ago. Her parents haven't heard from her since and they don't seem all that bothered.'

'Good work. Get her current address from the university.'

'I have, sir, but it's her parent's address.'

Bugger. Another dead end. But we now have a possible address where Janice could have been on the Saturday night, and where she probably ran from. Also, there is a potential whistle blower with useful information if we can get her to safety. Where was Margaret on the Saturday and Sunday nights?

CHAPTER NINETEEN

Six months before

The case of Regina v John Thomas Ramsey lasted for three weeks at Manchester Crown Court, but it took the jury just six hours to reach a verdict. Everyone in the courtroom heard the foreman of the jury say "guilty" very distinctly several times in answer to all the charges.

Ramsey's reaction was to turn in the direction of Inspector Max Cornell, point at him and mouth, "you're dead."

Cornell would have loved to have pointed back and mouth, "and you are going down with no remission," but just smiled instead. He may be wrong of course, the judge had yet to pass sentence.

It had been more of a contest than a trial. The defence argued that the video which quite clearly displayed one man shooting another, was fake. The prosecution produced a professional film maker who testified the video, although filmed on a smart phone, was not fake.

Then it was argued that the shooter in the video was not Ramsey, but an IT technician was called to "blow up" the face, which he did in in full view of the court and the identity of the pistol holder was clear for all to see.

As the murder weapon, said to be of 9mm calibre had not been found, the defence then suggested that despite the flash from the weapon as it was being fired and recorded on video, Ramsey had not actually fired the gun. "Good luck with that," said the lead prosecutor quietly, although many on the front bench, including the judge, heard the remark.

Then Cornell, when giving evidence, was subjected to a barrage of questions from the defence lawyers regarding Ramsey's illegal arrest and interviews under caution. Also, that the filming of the shooting had been set up by Cornell and was unlawful entrapment.

Cornell's comment of, "clutching at straws there, aren't we, counsellor?" earned him a rebuke from the judge.

The defence counsel argued vehemently that the video maker should be brought before the court as a witness, to examine his or her trustworthiness.

Cornell refused to identify the individual as he said it would put that person's life in danger. The defending lead barrister suggested he had watched too many American crime dramas. Cornell suggested that the defending barrister was incredibly naïve.

The judge asked Cornell if he genuinely

thought the video maker's life would be in danger.

Cornell replied that he didn't think it, he knew it. He was tempted, but refrained from mentioning the death of his wife as an example of what Ramsey was capable of.

The judge then made a proclamation.

'I can understand Inspector Cornell's reluctance to divulge the name of the video maker, but whether we know the identity of this person or not, it is still the job of the jury to decide whether the video is authentic or not, and if it is, is the man in the film actually shooting the other man and is the man performing the shooting John Thomas Ramsey? Knowing the identity of whoever recorded the event will not lessen this challenge.'

And so it was. Cornell kept secret the identity of the mother who had followed Ramsey unbeknown to him or his entourage, waiting for the chance to catch him committing a crime.

When that chance finally arrived, she stood in the shadows of a shop doorway adjacent to the night club, in the early hours of the morning and, using her smart phone camera, captured the shooting of a young man who had somehow come into conflict with the mobster.

The following day the mother walked into the main police station in Manchester and asked to speak to Inspector Max Cornell. The lady knew who to ask for recalling the news item reporting the death of his wife, a uniformed sergeant in the

Greater Manchester Police. The talk around town was that she had been killed by the mob as a warning to Cornell to back off.

***

Two days after the trial, at two o'clock in the morning, they came for him. Cornell knew they would. You cannot give evidence against the top thug in the area and not expect reprisals.

They were clumsy about it though. Cornell had purposely left a window open in the downstairs lounge and dozed in a chair with a blanket over himself, waiting.

After the first one had climbed in over the window sill and moved to allow his colleague in, Cornell put the barrel of the Glock against the first intruder's ear. The double click of the hammer being pulled back onto full cock caused both men to freeze.

'Don't think I won't shoot,' said Cornell. 'You killed my wife and you are now breaking into my house to kill me.'

Cornell reached inside the jacket of prowler number one and withdrew the weapon from the shoulder holster, telling him to do the same to his colleague then to pass the weapon over his shoulder.

Pointing weapons at both men's heads, Cornell ordered them to sit on the sofa and had them tie each other's wrists with cable ties, after which he called the police.

Within ten minutes his house was surrounded by a plethora of police cars and vans, the flashing blue lights casting huge shadows against the walls of the surrounding buildings. Neighbours appeared, donning dressing gowns to come out into their gardens and driveways to watch the show.

Cornell had the foresight to unlock his front door to allow easy access for a great many police, armed and dressed for battle.

Cornell knew the commander. He'd been on many raids with him.

'A little overkill, Ron, don't you think?' said Cornell. 'A couple of bobbies in a squad car would have done.'

'What have we got, Max?'

'Two of Ramsey's goons, come to pay me back for sending their boss down. Their two weapons are on the floor over by the window.'

'Anybody hurt?' asked the commander.

'Just their feelings,' said Cornell.

'This isn't going to stop, you know, Max.'

'I know,' he retorted.

***

'I know Michelle is buried here,' said Superintendent Sam McNestry the following morning, 'but you cannot remain in Manchester, Max. Ramsey's mob has tried once and they will try again. You have to move on.'

'You think they will give up if I move back to

London?' asked Cornell.

'They would be less likely to try it in another crime boss's jurisdiction. But there is also that opportunity in Newcastle to think about. It's promotion and while I'd be sorry to lose you, I certainly won't stand in your way.'

'Not usual for officers to move from one force to another, sir. Aren't the other inspectors bidding for promotion in Newcastle going to be upset if I move in over them?'

'Of course they will, but the Chief Constable up there wants someone with your experience; serious crime, murder in particular, and after I spoke to her, she wants you. Now, Newcastle has some distance to go to match Manchester for serious crime, but she doesn't have anyone with your expertise for north of the Tyne.'

CHAPTER TWENTY

Tuesday

The team, minus Donaldson, sat together in the incident room just as the low January sun reached the windows and necessitating the blinds to be drawn.

'Where's Donaldson?' asked Cornell, shrugging off his jacket.

'Rang in first thing, sir,' said Sergeant Harvey. 'She's gone to the university to see if she can identify any of the other girls Sadie referred to.'

'Good for her,' said Cornell. 'So, what about the car in Whittaker's garage?'

'Forensics found nothing unusual, sir. Margaret's DNA obviously, Janice's as well and two others, none of them on the database. One, possibly the driver who brought the car from Rothbury. Some evidence of marijuana, otherwise just sweet wrappers and cigarette ash on the floor.'

'Doesn't help us much, does it?' said Cornell.

'No, sir,' responded Bob Harvey. 'We could do a house to house around Whittaker's to see if anyone saw the car or the driver arrive, but

I'm not sure that would achieve anything, even if somebody did.'

Cornell was about to agree when his name was called.

'Sir, I have Inspector Lambert from Alnwick on line two,' interrupted an admin officer from across the floor.

Cornell picked up a receiver and punched digit two.

'Yes, Shaun?'

'Sir, I've just had Albert Henshaw on the blower. You know, the farmer who found Margaret Whitfield. Says there's four blokes walking around the hill where she was found. He reckons they are looking for something.'

'Whatever it is will probably be under the snow,' suggested Cornell.

'It's a bit milder today, sir. Snow's probably melting up there too. Do you want me to investigate? I can have somebody up there in twenty minutes.'

'You finished babysitting that MP?'

'Almost, sir. I'm driving him to Berwick tonight. A sergeant there is taking over from me.'

'OK. If you can spare a couple of uniforms, Shaun, find out what these chaps on the hill are looking for and whether they have found it.'

***

Cornell walked along the corridor to the gents and bumped into Chief Superintendent Mark

Braithwaite who was exiting.

'Afternoon, sir,' said Cornell enthusiastically.

'Huh, I understand you are no further forward in identifying Miss Whitfield's killer.'

'Oh! I wouldn't say that, sir. I think we are making progress,' said Cornell. 'We have Janice Whittaker's diaries.'

'I thought I told you not to…'

'I know, sir, but something came up and you were not around to consult. So I spoke to Judge Cornforth who gave me a warrant to search Whittaker's house and we found the diaries, which have some very interesting bits of information in them.'

L… Like what?' the superintendent stammered, his chief inspector's disobedience already forgotten.

'Possibly the identification of certain people, sir, any one of whom could be the murderer. And we now suspect there is something else, something big and nasty going on behind it all,' Cornell half lied.

He entered the gents leaving an open-mouthed superintendent standing in the corridor, his white face accentuating his five o' clock shadow with the most worried look on his face.

***

Cornell, pulling on his thick new anorak addressed his team.

'Right, you lot. I'm going to see the Crown Prosecution Service to find out more about Buffalo Bill Tierney's failed case. Bob, de-brief Donaldson when she gets back and follow up as appropriate and don't leave Janice's diaries unattended on a desk. I would hate for them to go missing.'

Bob Harvey gave his superior a strange look, then instructed Watkins to look after it.

***

'Need to speak to Mr Alistair McCormack, CPS,' Cornell said, showing the receptionist his ID.

'I'm afraid he's not taking visitors at the moment.'

'Is he in?' asked Cornell.

'Yes, he's just not taking visitors,' the receptionist responded, adding, 'I can make an appointment for you if you like, chief inspector.'

Why is everybody so bloody obstructive?

'I'll start again,' said Cornell. 'I need to speak to Alistair McCormack and I need to speak to him now and if you don't want to be arrested, handcuffed and taken into custody for obstructing the police, tell me which is his office.'

'Room 212 on the second floor.'

'Thank you. You have been most helpful. Don't ring him to announce my arrival, or I'll still arrest you.'

'Yes, sir. No, sir. I mean I won't, sir.'

Cornell took the steps to the second floor two at a time and found room 212. Cornell entered without knocking.

'Who the hell are you?' asked a seated and surprised Alistair McCormack.

'Detective Chief Inspector Max Cornell, Northumbria Police.' Cornell took out his ID card.

'How dare you just walk into my office!' shouted McCormack who had now risen to his feet, his facial colour changing to a purple hue.

'Sit down, Mr McCormack. We have something important to discuss.'

Cornell sat down in front of the desk.

'You will make a proper appointment if you want to discuss anything with me, chief inspector!'

'And I can handcuff you now and take you to the station for questioning regarding perverting the course of justice in the William Tierney case last year.'

McCormack's colour now changed to a paler pink, his demeanour suddenly less angry and a little more concerned. He sat back down with a thud.

'You were the prosecution counsel?' Cornell continued.

'I... I was,' McCormack stuttered.

'How did you lose the case? According to our case file notes, there was sufficient evidence and enough witnesses to send Tierney to the Tower.'

McCormack's head fell, then he put his head in his hands.

'Why do you want to know?' he asked slowly

and deliberately.

'We are investigating the suicide and murder of two girls; both probably sex workers and the evidence trail led us to the Tierney case. You will be able to work it out from there.'

'Oh, God!' uttered McCormack.

'From where I'm sitting, Mr McCormack, God isn't going to be much help to you. I'll ask you again; how did you lose that case? Either you tell me or I'll delve deeper, and something tells me you don't want me to go there.'

'I'm finished, aren't I?'

'Yes, so take some bad people down with you.'

'I should have a lawyer.'

'No, you shouldn't. Get a lawyer and you'll end up in jail, because he or she will tell you to keep stum. Tell me what went on with the Tierney case now, or I'll start an investigation into it first thing in the morning.'

'OK,' sighed McCormack. 'We had the evidence to begin with. That is why we agreed to prosecute. It was actually pretty cut and dried as you suggest, but when I got to court the first morning, I was informed by Chief Superintendent Braithwaite, who was the lead investigator, that my witnesses had gone missing.

'Then what?

'I got a call from Paul Whittaker asking to meet with him and his client. I thought it was to discuss the witness situation, but when I got to their room, Braithwaite was there too.'

'Go on,' prompted Cornell.

'Braithwaite told me I couldn't win the case, as there were no witnesses and the evidence had been tampered with, but I was to go through the motions anyway.'

'And you accepted. How much?'

'Excuse me?'

'How much did they pay you.'

'Look, I was faced with a case I couldn't win. I...'

'Why didn't you call the police?' demanded Cornell.

'I didn't go to the police because Braithwaite was the police.'

'Tell me, Mr McCormack, why do you think Whittaker and Braithwaite got into bed with a known criminal?'

'I think they were offered something by Tierney which was too good to ignore. And in return for this favour, they would allow the case to go south. I have no proof of that, it is just a feeling formed on what I observed.'

'What do you think they were offered?'

'I haven't a clue, chief inspector. Something lucrative but unlawful I have no doubt.'

'So, what are you going to do now, Mr McCormack?'

'I will resign immediately.'

'That's a good idea. I really think you should, in fact I insist on it. I should also arrest you, but if

I do, Chief Superintendent Braithwaite will get to know about it very quickly and alert a murderer, as well as covering up whatever he and Whittaker are involved in.'

'So, what are you going to do, chief inspector?'

'I'm going to walk away, Mr McCormack. You will write your resignation, then ride off into the sunset. The Canaries are very nice this time of year, I'm told. Please do not commit suicide or attempt to contact Braithwaite or Whittaker. That would not do at all.'

**

Laura Donaldson had returned from the university. Bob Harvey had de-briefed her, but suggested she explain what she had discovered to Cornell.

The university had been unusually co-operative and had given Donaldson five names of other female students who were friendly with Janice and Margaret. One was Sadie Tomkinson who was absent from university, as was another, but Donaldson saw the other three.

Two clammed up and wouldn't say a word but the other, when she had finished pleading with Donaldson not to tell her parents, said that they worked part time for a club, but refused to say what kind of club it was.

Donaldson asked if she and the others were sex workers for this club, but she wouldn't admit to it. *Hardly surprising.* The student added that their lives were in danger if they said anything to anybody, most of all the police. She refused to say who owned the club, or indeed how she thought their lives were in danger.

'Laura, do you think that if we got these students in here individually, away from the university scene and each other, they would talk to us?' asked Harvey.

'You mean frighten the shite out of them, sarge?' contributed an eager and grinning Ian Dennison.

'No, sarge,' replied Donaldson, ignoring her colleague's frivolous remark. 'They are more frightened of this club, whatever it is, than the police.'

'A sex business,' suggested David Watkins. 'That's what we are dealing with here, I'll bet. By the way, sir, Chief Superintendent Braithwaite was looking around our desks while you were out. He seemed to be looking for something, but I don't think he found it.'

'Thanks, David. I take it you put Janice's diaries out of sight of probing eyes?'

'Yes, sir,' answered a perplexed David Watkins.

'Bob,' Cornell turned to his sergeant, 'you were looking at Whittaker's bank accounts.'

'Sir. Paul Whittaker's account only showed he was well off. Not much coming in these last few months but before that there were large amounts going in, albeit at irregular intervals. We could check but I suspect they were bone fide legal fee payments. If he is earning anything at the moment, it's in a bank account we are not aware of. Is there anyone else you would like me to check up on, sir?'

'Not at the moment, Bob.'

'Sir,' asked Harvey, 'what are we looking at here? A club of girls for hire, using premises in Herrington? That address you gave me to look up?'

'It's what it's looking like, Bob. A club, or, as Watkins assumed correctly, a sex business. A sex business that terrifies its girls into obedience, but when one breaks the silence, bad things happen. I think I know who is behind it, but I need a bit more evidence before I can start throwing names around. Do we know who owns the craft shop and upstairs yet?'

'The registry hasn't been back yet. I'll chase them up.'

'Threaten them, Bob.'

***

Late in the day Cornell's mobile rang, the display showing Inspector Shaun Lambert calling.

'Yes, Shaun.'

'Sir, my lads have just rung in from visiting Albert Henshaw. Those guys he saw up the hill have long gone, but Albert and his dog decided to go and have a look for themselves, and guess what?'

'His dog found a stash of gold coins.'

'You've got it,' Lambert joked. 'No, sir. The dog has actually found a mobile phone. Sir, we should hire this dog. It's got more intelligence than most police officers.'

'Don't belittle the lower ranks, inspector,' cautioned Cornell.

'It wasn't the lower ranks I was referring to, sir.'

'Do you know if the phone is alright? Can your boys get into it?'

'Seems fine apart from the dog's teeth marks on the screen and the battery has run down. The lads have put it on their car's charger, but there's an access code which someone has changed from the usual 1111.'

'Where are your lads now, Shaun?'

'In in a layby more or less opposite that new house that's been built just off the Rothbury Road along from Henshaw's, and they've just told me something very interesting, sir.'

'What's that?'

'They are sure they saw Kool Stinger leaving the building and getting into a Porsche. When he noticed the police car opposite, he shot off in a cloud of dust.'

'Who the hell is Kool Stinger, Shaun?'

'A popular rapper, sir. I think he's African American. Always wears white suits. I think his real name is Kojo something. He's had a couple of big hits.'

'Very interesting, Shaun. A rich kid with a guilty conscience. Just make sure your boys get that phone back to you in one piece, then you sleep with it and bring it to forensics first thing tomorrow.'

So, it's looking like a sex ring, possibly owned and operated by Whittaker and Braithwaite, operating out of Herrington and possibly somewhere else. Using a dozen girls, some of whom are students, one the daughter of Whittaker. But a lot of this is just supposition. Still no further forward in finding a murderer and time is getting on.

CHAPTER
TWENTY ONE

Wednesday

'Please tell me your guys have got into that mobile phone Shaun Lambert brought in, Mabel,' said Cornell, hanging his coat on an empty peg then ordering a black coffee. Both he and the forensics pathologist were meeting for lunch at a popular café, midway between their places of work. Afterwards, Cornell was meeting with the chief constable.

'Give them a chance, Max. Apparently there's an app securing the access and it is ten times more difficult to break into than the phone's own security.'

'I seem to be taking two steps forward and three back all the time as far as discovering who murdered Margaret Whitfield. On the other hand, I've possibly uncovered a sex business which may be owned and managed by high profile people, whose identities, you simply wouldn't believe.'

Laura Donaldson knew better than to ask who. If Cornell had wanted her to know he would have given her the names.

'Ooh! How exciting! Do you think the murderer could be one of them?'

'I don't think so, but I'm confident that those involved will know, or at the very least suspect who the murderer is.'

'Do you think Paul Whittaker knew what his daughter was up to?'

'I think Paul Whittaker definitely did. I can't say too much at the moment, Mabel, but I think Whittaker, his daughter, and her friend were involved with this sex business, but I have no evidence.'

'Oh, how repugnant is that?'

'Yeah! I think repugnant sums it up.'

'Speaking of daughters, my daughter is coming home tomorrow,' said Wainwright, deftly changing the subject. 'I would like the two of you to meet.'

'I saw what you did there,' answered Cornell. 'That's fine. We'll fix something up when I've got some time.'

Bloody hell. This is starting to get serious, isn't it? Meeting the family now? Hell, we are not even girlfriend/boyfriend.

***

Chief Constable Mary Dewsbury lifted her receiver and punched a digit.

'No calls until I tell you otherwise,' she said into the mouth piece, then she dropped the receiver back on to its cradle.

Across the desk from her was Detective Chief Inspector Max Cornell, there to answer questions as to why no arrests in the murder of Margaret Whitfield had yet been made.

'I'm at a dinner tonight, Max, local dignitaries and leaders of various institutions, all with influence and I don't want to appear ignorant if I'm asked the question. So put me in the picture.'

'Yes, ma'am. I'll start with Janice Whittaker. I don't know if she was murdered, but I think she was physically abused before she ran to her death. I do know Margaret Whitfield was murdered, but I do not yet know who murdered her.'

Cornell went on to explain how he thought Paul Whittaker and Mark Braithwaite had acquired a sex business from William Tierney in return for the collapse of his murder trial, but he had no evidence to back it up other than a notion of the CPS prosecutor, and his own observations.

'Whoever the murderer is,' added Cornell, 'he is very likely to be a client of this business which provides sexual favours for the rich and famous.'

'And you think these capital letters in the diaries are initials?' asked the chief constable, who was scanning a photocopied list.

'Yes, ma'am, and as you can see, there are about two dozen different sets.'

'And you think they belong to whom?'

'The clientele, ma'am. The punters in this

sex business.'

'Why do you say that?'

'It would fit, ma'am. They occur in the diaries only at weekends. I think the sets of initials on a particular date refer to Janice's client, or clients, for that night. Unfortunately, those listed for the Saturday she died do not mean anything to us.'

'Why just at weekends?'

'Janice was a student, ma'am. She would have been at university during the week, at least until she dropped out. Then presumably she didn't bother to change her working pattern. I don't know more than that.'

'Have you identified anyone from any of the initials?'

'We think the SK is Simon Kane, quiz show host, who was seen going in to the Herrington building by Constable Hargreaves. The same with Stuart Turner, prominent rock bass guitarist, but no one else.'

'My God, what is this world coming to? But this won't stand up in court, will it, Max?' responded the chief constable. 'These people are not going to admit why they were really entering a craft shop on a Sunday night, are they? I could think of a number of innocent reasons for doing so.'

'I agree, we need more, but it's a start.'

'Also, I can't allow Braithwaite to carry on in his position if he is involved in running an escort business, and you can't interview him as he is entitled to be interviewed by a rank above himself. I will either have to do it myself or bring someone in, which will take ages to arrange and word will get out.' She paused, noticing the look on Cornell's face. 'You don't look as if you think that's the best thing to do.'

'Two things, ma'am. If we are implicating a chief superintendent in a sex crime, we need substantial evidence, which I haven't got, and two, I'm worried it will blow the whole case apart. Ma'am, the punters are wealthy celebrities. If they are alerted that we are on to them they will disappear, the murderer included, and I don't mean to distant parts of the UK.'

'I know, but at the same time my arse won't touch the ground if it gets out that I allowed a senior police officer to continue working, suspecting what he is involved with.'

'I need more time, ma'am. Time to find a murderer.'

'I will stick my neck out, Max. You can have twenty-four hours then he's suspended. If that impedes the murder investigation, then I'm sorry, but I have no alternative.'

***

Cornell drove home after his meeting. He was tired; he hadn't slept much since Janice had been found.

This was his third murder since he'd moved

back to the North East, but the previous two cases had been easy by comparison. Both involved drink.

The first was a knife attack outside a pub in the west end of Newcastle. Two mates arguing over one girl. Sergeant Bob Harvey knew the attacker from the description given by witnesses, and the blood found on his knife matched the victim's.

The second murder occurred when a group of four lads were sitting in a pub before going to the match. One of them, disagreeing with his brother over Newcastle United's current tactics, punched his sibling on the temple once. Just once, and according to the pathologist, it caused an epidural haematoma from which he died the following day. It hadn't been a hard punch, but it was in front of a pub-load of witnesses.

***

As he walked up the path to his front door looking forward to a shower then bed, his next-door neighbour, Mrs Nicholson, opened her door and was holding back, with difficulty, her German Shepherd, Rex.

'I wonder if you could take him for a bit walk, Max? He's not been out all day. I've not been well and just couldn't manage it. Could you?'

'Yes, I'll just put my gear in the house. Not be a minute.'

'Bless you, Max, 'said Mrs Nicholson, then turning her attention to the dog. 'Now you be a good boy for Uncle Max, won't you?'

***

The dog had grown much larger than a German Shepherd had a right to be and Cornell wondered why a woman in her late eighties would want a German Shepherd for a companion.

She'd told Max it was an eight week old pup when she had bought him two years ago. She thought his feet were unusually large at the time but didn't think it was a sign the dog would grow so big. It seemed like a good idea to get a pet dog, for company. And she felt safe with him around.

Cornell didn't doubt the latter. He had asked her why she hadn't gone for something smaller, like a Rottweiler, or one of those Japanese Mastiffs which were about the size of a small pony. She had laughed and said no, her German Shepherd would do.

Nevertheless, she had trained the dog well. He sat when you told him to and he came when you called.

This wasn't the first time he had taken his "nephew" for a stroll along the beach of Cullercoats and despite his tiredness, Cornell enjoyed the fresh air.

CHAPTER TWENTY TWO

Thursday

They were good, whoever they were, thought Cornell. Using a not too small, dark coloured, popular car, following immediately behind him one day, then two cars behind him on another. Today, the vehicle was parked across the street from the station, like it was two days ago, but now in a different parking spot.

Yes, they were good, but was it they, or he/she? Were there other cars involved that he hadn't noticed? Was the car he was looking at now a decoy?

Was it Ramsey's mob from the north west coming after him again? Could it be Tierney's mob watching him for whatever reason?

What about Braithwaite? If everything Cornell thought he was involved with were true, he would know the Newcastle underworld pretty well now.

Had Braithwaite organised a hit?

All these possibilities were going through

Cornell's mind as he stood at the window of the incident room, drinking his first works coffee of the day and looking out across one of Newcastle's busiest streets.

If he'd not worked for special branch, or anti-terror, he would never have been trained in surveillance and would probably not have realised he was being followed now.

'Sir,' said Bob Harvey from the other side of the incident room, 'forensics have got into that mobile phone and it turns out to be Margaret Whitfield's.'

Cornell quickly turned his attention to his sergeant.

'You're joking. I didn't expect that.'

'Why not, sir?' asked Harvey.

'Because I don't think she was murdered up on the moor and neither does Doc Wainwright. You don't think to take your mobile with you when you're dead.'

'So how did it get there, sir?'

'The only thing I can think of, Bob, is that whoever dumped her body also had her phone with him and lost it.

'It's possible,' adjudged Harvey.

'Anyway, find anything interesting on it?'

'Calls, apart from the last two days of her life, had been deleted. We can get them back, but it will take a while. So, we have been on to the provider who has given us the phone record for the last six months. Lots of calls between Margaret and another mobile which could have been Janice's. I rang it, but got the unavailable tone. Other calls to the same people repeated. We will need a warrant to discover their identities, or we ring them and hope they give themselves away. But, sir, Dennison found something very interesting. I'll let him tell you.'

'Sir,' said Dennison, 'there was one number amongst those calls Margaret received but hadn't deleted. I thought I recognised it, sir.'

'I'm listening, Ian,' said Cornell.

'Sir, before I came to this team, I was a patrol car driver.'

'From what I heard, Ian, that's debatable, but carry on.'

There was some laughter and Dennison moved uneasily in his seat at the reference to his abuses of police transport.

'Sir, there was an occasion when Chief Superintendent Braithwaite asked me to drive him, in his car, to some kind of lunchtime bash and pick him up later in the afternoon when he rang me. I saved the number on my phone in case he asked me again, sir.'

'And?'

'Margaret Whitfield received a call from that mobile on Sunday 6th January at fifteen hundred hours, sir.'

There were intakes of breath, followed by a deathly silence in the incident room. All eyes were on DCI Cornell wondering what his response would be.

He sat on the edge of a desk to address the team.

'OK, here we go. This is what I think. About eight months ago, Buffalo Bill Tierney was charged with sex crimes and murder. Chief Investigating Officer was none other than Detective Chief Superintendent Mark Braithwaite. CPS prosecutor was Alasdair McCormack and the defence barrister, Paul Whittaker QC.

'You all know what happened with that case; it fell over. It's the ex-chief CPS prosecutor's belief that Braithwaite and Whittaker accepted some kind of offer from Buffalo Bill in return for evidence to go astray and witnesses to disappear. It is my belief that the offer was a lucrative sex business. However, I have no proof, only bits of evidence that appear to fall into place. In view of that, I would appreciate it if that information doesn't leave these four walls for now.'

All of the team sat with incredulous looks on their faces, learning of the possible involvement of their chief superintendent in an illegal sex business. Cornell continued.

'The business was increased in size after Braithwaite and Whittaker took control of it by recruiting several female students, one of whom was Whittaker's own daughter and another, her friend.'

'How can anybody do that?' asked Dennison with disdain.

No one answered because there was no answer. However, it prompted a question from Watkins.

'Why would students agree to become prostitutes, sir?'

'This wasn't a street operation,' interjected Bob Harvey. 'It wasn't pimps and tarts where a lot of the girls are on the game to pay for a heroin habit. This was high class escort stuff. Wealthy celebrities, who would pay four figure amounts; students seeing pound signs before their eyes, fees paid. Why do you think they did it?'

'I agree,' said Cornell. 'Thanks for that, Bob. In addition to increasing their productive labour force, I believe heavies or minders were also recruited, sufficient to manage and threaten the girls to keep them in their place.'

'Do you think one of these minders murdered Margaret Whitfield?' asked Watkins.

'Or, Chief Superintendent Braithwaite?' advanced Dennison.

'Neither Superintendent Braithwaite nor Paul Whittaker fit Doc Wainwright's profile of the murderer being a very tall man. I think it's more likely to be one of the punters. Perhaps someone whose demands were out of the ordinary. One of the minders could have been responsible for Janice's death, if she was chased from Herrington High Street to the harbour, as we think she was.'

'Why Herrington?' asked Watkins. 'And I wouldn't have thought the rear of a craft shop would be a conducive venue for the purposes of sex.'

'It would seem sensible to have such a venue away from the city, David, and Herrington is as good a place as any, and I think a craft shop is an excellent front. I have no doubt the business was being conducted upstairs, which I believe extends over the property next door. However, I'm equally sure there must also have been somewhere else to utilise all the girls.

'You make it sound like a factory production line, sir,' complained Donaldson.

'I do, don't I?'

'Are we going to raid those premises, sir?' asked Dennison.

'Yes, when the time is right.'

'So, what do we do now, sir?' asked Donaldson.

'Two important things. One, I want Sadie Tomkinson found. I still think her life is in danger as she could have important information for us. Bob, you and David on that. Secondly, those initials Janice had written down for the Saturday night; Ian, any ideas at all?'

'One set leapt out at us, sir.'

'Carry on.'

'There was one set she had not written down anywhere else in her diaries before the Saturday, sir, and she had also put the same initials down for the Sunday as well.'

Cornell looked at his list and Dennison

pointed them out.

'This means that the Saturday is the first occasion she was to meet this particular client with these initials.'

'Yes, sir. I'll bet if we can put a name to them, we will find our murderer, sir.'

'I agree, so get on with it then.'

***

Cornell sat at his office desk speaking on the phone to Mabel Wainwright. He was being invited to Sunday lunch to meet Marian, the daughter, when a pencil bounced off his partition window.

He stood and saw Bob Harvey on the phone, signalling to him.

'I have to go,' he said, after hastily accepting the invitation. He would think about his hastiness later.

'Alright, Sadie. Can you tell me where you are?' said Harvey speaking into the phone. 'I know, Sadie, but it's for your own protection,' he added. 'OK, Sadie, just say what you want to tell me.'

Harvey grabbed his A4 notepad and pencil and began taking notes. After what seemed like a minute of scribbling, Harvey spoke again. 'That's very helpful, Sadie. Now, can you get to somewhere safe? Sadie! Sadie! She's rung off, sir.'

Cornell turned the A4 pad towards him to read the notes.

Janice's dad and high up copper own business.
So called bodyguards run it. One of them, Kurt

was leader. Right bastard. Sometimes hit us So do clients some badly Not much of a life Money good but have to fight Kurt for it. Herrington used to be main place opened another somewhere else. Others going to be opened.

> *frightened one girl beaten up answering back*
> *Margaret Janice wanted out*
> *they said would tell threatened*

'It's a bit jumbled, sir. I can write it out properly.'

'Yes, do that sergeant, but I get the drift. Tried to trace the call?'

'Watkins asked IT, sir. They are looking at the computer now, however, it was from a call box.'

'Call box? Didn't think we had them anymore. They're extinct aren't they,' commented Cornell.

'Call was from Sunderland, sir,' shouted Dennison across the room. There were some smirks from the others.

'Don't,' admonished Cornell, who was well aware of the rivalry between the two cities and the banter that went with it. Then a thought flashed through his mind. 'Bob, that new house near Rothbury. Damn, I missed the connection when Lambert told me. A couple of his officers saw some rapper guy, Cool somebody, coming out of that house.'

'Kool Stinger, sir, with a K,' piped up Dennison.

'Right. That was him. Anyway, he was

wearing a white suit. Hargreaves said he saw a black guy in a white suit going into the Herrington craft shop.' Cornell glanced at his watch. Five fifteen, too late today. 'Bob, first thing tomorrow, find out who owns that Rothbury house. Watkins, try and track down this Kurt.'

***

Cornell left his office at six o'clock.

No one seemed to follow him home. After he disposed of his work suit, it was his intention to go for a pint, get a takeaway and watch some tele if he could get the case out of his head for a few hours.

Approaching his front entrance, he heard Mrs Nicholson's dog Rex barking next door. That was unusual. Rex barked when you knocked on the door, but only then. Mrs Nic had him really well trained. The barking did not let up as Cornell opened his front door.

Both he and Mrs Nic had the keys to each other's homes so Cornell retrieved Mrs Nic's set and entered her house. He found Mrs Ethel Nicholson sitting in her arm chair, eyes wide open and staring straight ahead at nothing. She was dead.

Cornell closed her eyes, then let the dog out into the garden, to its great relief, then phoned for an ambulance.

He informed the operator that the lady was quite dead and had been for some hours. How did he know? Well, he was a policeman and had seen many deaths and had observed that when their bodies are cold and blue with no pulse, they are most often, dead.

He added that there appeared nothing suspicious about the death, but he would phone the local police.

He made that his next phone call. He was told to stay at the house until the police arrived and no, they couldn't say when that would be as they were busy and would get there when they could.

So, Cornell told them he was a DCI and if they didn't have a uniform at the address in fifteen minutes, someone's head would roll. A police car arrived under a siren within five minutes and before the paramedics.

Cornell produced his warrant card on request. Then the ambulance arrived and the paramedics pronounced Mrs Nic dead. As she was eighty nine and had not been well the day before, she most likely had died of natural causes. The coroner would decide whether a post mortem was required.

As the ambulance drove away with Mrs Nic, his neighbour on the other side came to the door.

'Is that Mrs Nic?' Jennifer Laidlaw asked.

'It is, Jenny. She's dead, I'm afraid.'

'Oh! That's awful news. I only spoke to her yesterday, but she did seem awfully frail. She was eighty nine, you know.'

'I know.'

'What about the dog?'

'I'll look after him until someone turns up. She had children, didn't she?'

'Yes, I think so.'

'Well, they will probably want him.'

'If they don't, I think you should have him, Max. I could help, I couldn't take the dog on full time, but I could look after him when you are at work.'

'That would be fine, Jenny, if it works out that way.'

He collected the dog's huge bed, dishes, biscuits and dog food from Mrs Nicholson's kitchen and took them and the dog into his house.

He fed the dog, after which it drank some water then lay down in front of the imitation coal gas fire. Cornell's mobile rang.

'Cornell,' he answered.

'Sir, just had Doctor Wainwright on the phone,' said Sergeant Bob Harvey. 'She's attending a possible murder scene at South Shields.'

'What's that got to do with us, Bob?'

'Doc Wainwright thinks it's the same killer as did for Margaret Whitfield, sir. And from her description, I think the body could be Sadie Tomkinson.'

'Shit,' said Cornell. 'Do we know who the attending crime officer is?'

'Doc Wainwright says it's an Inspector Mary Stewart and she's arrested two boys who found the body, on suspicion.'

'Christ, this is getting worse. Whereabouts in South Shields, Bob?' asked Cornell.

'On the beach, sir.'

'Get over there now. I'll take the ferry from North Shields. If I catch it right, should be with you within the hour.'

Cornell grabbed his coat and the dog's leash.

'Come on, son. This is your first case.' Rex jumped to his feet in anticipation.

Once in the car the dog sat in the front passenger seat like a human passenger, the seat belt under his front legs, across his body. Cornell had a brief vision of the dog wearing a police helmet which made him chuckle.

Leaving his car parked, Cornell and dog were fortunate to board the ferry just as it was embarking.

***

Max Cornell showed his ID to the officer patrolling the tape which had been positioned around the pathologist's tent covering the body on the beach. The generator powering the searchlight was throbbing away unseen in the shadow of the tent.

'Where's Sergeant Harvey?' Cornell asked the officer.

'He's over there, sir,' the officer said, pointing at a custody van parked on the roadside next to the beach. He's trying to talk to the young lads who found the body, but our inspector is having none of it.'

Cornell sighed as he looked over. He saw four people standing by the custody van, highlighted by a street lamp.

'Hold my dog, will you?'

Cornell gave the leash to the officer and headed over the beach to where Harvey and the inspector and two uniforms were in attendance.

As he got closer, Bob Harvey spotted him when he came into view under the street light.

'Sir, help me out here,' cried Harvey.

'Who are you?' demanded a young lady standing with hands on hips.

'DCI Max Cornell. Who are you?'

'Oh,' exclaimed the lady. 'Inspector Mary Stewart, I'm in charge here.'

'So why are you arguing with my sergeant?'

'He wants to interview my suspects and that is not his job. There is no reason for him to be here.'

'I hate to have to pull rank on you, inspector, but I want my sergeant to speak to your so-called suspects. Officer,' Cornell said to the nearest uniform, 'get these lads out of that van. Go ahead Bob. Inspector, you come with me.'

'I don't seem to have much choice, do I?'

'No inspector. You don't.'

Cornell set off across the sand towards the pathologist's tent with the rather subdued Inspector Stewart in tow.

He entered the tent and held the flap open for the inspector.

'What have you got, Mabel?' asked Cornell.

'Oh, thank God you are here. This lass has arrested the two young men who found the body and refused to listen to what I had to say. I thought if I didn't call you in, we would lose something.'

'You did right, Mabel. Thanks. Sergeant Harvey is interviewing the two lads now.'

'Good. So, here we have a woman of about nineteen or twenty. Strangled within the last two to three hours, much the same way as Margaret Whitfield. A very strong man using just one hand. His left. Look, can you see the marks? See that one there? That's his thumb.'

'Quite clear, aren't they?' reflected Cornell.

'That's because they are fresh. They will fade in time, but we have the photos. The girl has no ID and is not wearing shoes, although she is wearing a lightweight anorak. No phone, a ten pound note on her and some change.'

'She's called Sadie Tomkinson, Mabel. A working colleague of Janice and Margaret. She was trying to blow the whistle on the operation but had to go on the run. She spoke to my office this afternoon from Sunderland, then obviously didn't run fast enough. There will be footprints won't there?'

'There are plenty, Max, and there is evidence of a struggle around the body, but the sand here is very dry. The tide hasn't reached this high up the beach for a few days and the sun has been out all day, so there are no discernible footprints.'

Cornell and Stewart left the tent.

'I'm sorry, sir. I didn't realise,' the inspector said, somewhat restrained.

'A bit of advice, inspector. You only become a detective when you listen to people, such as experts like Doc Wainwright, and witnesses. These two lads you've arrested; they phoned in the discovery of the body, which they probably wouldn't have done if they'd murdered her. Nor would they have stayed in the vicinity.'

'I just thought I should treat them as suspects.'

'Less likely to talk to you if you handcuff them and lock them up in a bloody van.'

'I'm sorry again, sir.'

'OK, so, let's go and see what they have to say.'

They walked back towards the custody van, Cornell collecting his dog on the way.

'Nice dog, sir,' said the officer. 'As good as gold. Just sitting there, waiting for you. He's a big bugger though, isn't he?'

'Thanks, officer. I think he's stopped growing,' said Cornell, stroking the dog's head and hoping that Mrs Nic's offspring were not into large animals. He quite liked the idea of owning a big German Shepherd.

'Sir, found a shoe by the wall over there and another over here.'

The officer produced a pair of leather shoes with a semi high heel, holding them up with his little fingers. 'They may have been the girl's, sir. She could have kicked her shoes off in order to run on the sand.'

'Good man. Get them bagged.'

At the custody van, the two boys looked terrified as they answered Harvey's questions. He had removed their handcuffs.

'Sir, these two lads saw two men leaving the scene.'

Cornell's attention heightened. He looked over the two. They were both about sixteen or seventeen and desperately trying, but failing to hold back their breath from Harvey so he wouldn't smell the beer fumes.

Also, stumbling over a body which had only died moments before, then arrested, handcuffed and placed in police custody, had done little to improve their anxiety.

'Can they describe these two men?' asked Cornell.

'They say both men were tall, one much taller than the other. The shorter of the two was thickset, looked like a boxer. They ran off fast in that direction.' Harvey pointed northwards.

'Did you hear them say anything?' asked Cornell addressing the two boys.

'No, sir. They gave us both a shock when they came running out of the darkness and I think our presence shocked them. We wondered what they were running from so we walked over and that was when we found the body.'

'Can I ask why you were on the beach tonight?' asked Cornell.

They looked at each other sheepishly.

'We've both been selected to play football for Earlinston first team this Saturday, so we went out to celebrate. We had a bit too much and somehow ended up on the beach.'

Cornell looked at Harvey, who shook his head, then took both their addresses and commended them for their actions.

'Are we in trouble?' one asked.

'No,' replied Harvey, 'but best if you wait until you are eighteen before you celebrate again and perhaps you should refrain from informing your team manager about your little escapade tonight.'

The two boys walked off towards the town.

'You are letting them go?' questioned Inspector Stewart.

'Whenever there's a murder, Inspector Stewart, it's better not arresting the first people you meet, or the person who finds the body, as they may have some important information. We were lucky that your impulsion to imprison them didn't shut them up.'

'Didn't know you had a dog, sir,' stated Harvey.

'Neither did I until tonight, Bob.'

Cornell explained about his next-door neighbour's demise as they walked over to where the boys had said the tall men had run.

The sand was firm here where the last tide had reached, and there in the torch light of Harvey's smartphone, were two sets of footprints. One set were very large footprints.

'Don't move so I can find you again,' said Cornell. 'Here, hold the dog.'

Cornell trotted quickly over to the forensics tent.

'Mabel, do you have anything to take a cast of a footprint?'

'Tom here can do it,' Wainwright referred to her assistant. 'Why, have you found one?'

'Found a few and one set are bloody huge.'

Wainwright smiled.

'That's our man.'

Another murder. Big, tall man seen running away. Big, tall man strangled Margaret. Is it the same big, tall man? Who the hell is he? We have his size, his initials, even his footprints. But what's his bloody name?

CHAPTER TWENTY THREE

Friday

After speaking to his counterpart for south of the Tyne to account for and clear the reason he and his sergeant were in South Shields the night before, Cornell rang his chief constable.

'Ma'am, there was another murder last night, I believe committed by the same guy as murdered Margaret Whitfield, so hold back on suspending Braithwaite. I still have no solid evidence to suggest he's involved anyway,' appealed DCI Max Cornell to the chief constable.

'Can't take the risk, Max, I've told you that already. If the press gets hold of this, I'm toast. I have to suspend him right away.'

Cornell took a deep breath.

'Ma'am, there's a killer out there who's murdered two girls and possibly caused the death of a third, and will probably kill again if he feels threatened. That concerns me more than your reputation at this precise moment in time, ma'am. If you suspend Braithwaite now, the murderer could disappear, or make it damned difficult for us to find him.'

There was a pause which probably only lasted a few seconds but to Cornell it seemed to last for many minutes. However, the response was less caustic than he thought it would be.

'Your former superiors told me you speak your mind and have little regard for authority,' the chief constable said finally, and with some menace.

'What would you prefer me to say, ma'am?'

She changed to subject.

'Are you anywhere nearer identifying this murderer?'

'Closer. We have his footprints and his initials. Just need to put a name to them.'

'I will give you until tomorrow night. Whatever else happens, Braithwaite goes first thing Sunday morning.'

'Thank you, ma'am.'

'And DCI Cornell, don't you ever ....,' but Cornell had rung off.

***

Cornell would never have done this in Manchester, but he believed Newcastle was different. He was going to meet the area's crime boss, William Buffalo Bill Tierney. He needed to be sure that Mark Braithwaite and Paul Whittaker were co-owners of this sex business.

You can only take speculation so far. He

knew Tierney would never agree to give evidence, but confirming the suspicion would be enough for now.

It was not difficult to find the mobster's home address on Darras Hall estate, where many of Tyneside's wealthy lived.

However, according to the woman who answered the door smoking a cigarette in a holder, Mr Tierney was not at home. During the day, she informed Cornell, he liked to check up on his public houses, and today he was at the "Monk's Retreat" in Jesmond.

***

Cornell drove to Jesmond wondering where the monastery was that gave the pub its name. On arrival he parked up and walked into the lounge. At the bar he asked for Mr Tierney. Seconds later security appeared at his side.

The usual broken nose, scar tissue around the eyes, but smartly dressed in a bow tie, nevertheless.

'You are asking for Mr Tierney?' security man asked.

'Yes,' replied Cornell. 'And I'm not armed,' he added smiling, as the bodyguard looked him up and down, eyes searching for the tell-tale bulge under the shoulder or at the hip.

'And whom shall I say is asking for him?'

'DCI Max Cornell, Newcastle MIT.'

The man visibly flinched. He had not

expected that declaration.

'And your business?'

'None of yours,' Cornell responded, no longer smiling and finding the continuous questioning tiresome. He stared unblinking into the bodyguard's eyes.

The man turned about and approached a table where three men were seated. All three looked at Cornell standing leaning against the bar. One of them stared at him longer than the others trying to place the visitor, and ruminating as to whether he should grant Cornell's request.

Finally, he nodded. The bodyguard returned to Cornell as Tierney waved his two guests away from his table.

'He will see you,' said the bodyguard.

Cornell left the bar and walked over. There was a television nearby, the sound turned down but still audible enough to drown the conversation from the table.

'DCI Max Cornell,' said Tierney thoughtfully. 'Why do I not know that name?'

'I'm new here, Mr Tierney, from Manchester. I worked serious crime over there until I'd put them all away and had nothing else left to do.'

Tierney didn't bat an eyelid.

'And do I need to be concerned about this visit, chief inspector?'

'Mr Tierney, today I am seeking information. Tomorrow depends on you.'

'What information could I possibly have

that would be of interest to Detective Chief Inspector Max Cornell, did you say?'

'About eight/nine months ago you were in court charged with serious crimes. The evidence subsequently went missing and the witnesses disappeared, or developed amnesia, so you walked.'

'You've done your homework, chief inspector.'

'The reason why the prosecution's case fell apart is because you got to the lead police officer and your defence counsel, and made them an offer they couldn't refuse.'

'Go on, chief inspector.'

'You offered them an established and lucrative sex business; a dozen or so girls thrown in.'

'If you know all this, why are you asking me?' enquired the crime boss.

'My problem is I don't know it, Mr Tierney. I'm pretty sure it's true, but if it's not I could end up back walking the beat. It would help me if you would confirm it.'

'And why would I do that?'

'Why not? You are not subject to a current police investigation, so what does it matter to you? It could also assist us with the investigations into the murders of a couple of the girls working for said sex business. I appeal to your civic duty.'

'Three girls have died, I hear,' said Tierney.

'Yes, Mr Tierney. One may have committed

suicide or perhaps in panic jumped into icy cold waters, but two were definitely murdered. I am investigating their deaths. All three were involved in a business we think is owned by a police superintendent and a barrister. A business which I believe they acquired from you.'

'And you want me to confirm this, chief inspector?'

'Mr Tierney. The sale of a sex business such as this is not illegal, but the operation of one is. I am not after you today, Mr Tierney.'

'Chief Inspector, can I assume you are not wired?'

'I am not wired, Mr Tierney. You have my word.'

'Then, your summation is not incorrect, chief inspector.'

Cornell had to think about the double negative for a second or two.

Wasn't saying he was right, just not wrong.

'You any idea who the murderer of these girls is, Mr Tierney?'

'From what I hear from my people, chief inspector, you should be casting your net wider than the local area.'

Now how does he know that? Don't press him. He isn't going to mention the murderer's name, even if he does know it, but he probably doesn't.

'Thank you, Mr Tierney.'

'You will have a drink with me, chief inspector?'

Now that is a surprise, but why the hell not?

'Yes, I will. Thank you. A pint of bitter will do very nicely.'

Tierney raised his hand to get the barman's attention and signalled for service. He then turned his attention to the television which was currently showing the news. The remote was on the table in front of him and he increased the volume.

'Don't you get sick of this Brexit business,' said Tierney.

Cornell had to agree. He and most likeminded individuals were sick to death of the Brexit debate which still hogged most of the headlines as it had done for the last three years. Tierney was obviously a Tory and although politically neutral, Cornell found his comments not too contrary.

The local bulletin followed as Cornell had drunk past the half way point of his pint. Tierney was even more absorbed with news items from his own back yard.

A local village infant school planting trees on a village green; a branch of the Mother's Union returning from a trip to Buckingham Palace seemed to captivate him.

Finally, that Member of Parliament being interviewed by the same reporter as the last time, thanking everyone involved for making his two week fact finding mission to Northumberland and the Borders so pleasant and constructive. This was despite the weather, he joked, holding up his gloved hands. Yeah, and taking up police resources, Cornell recollected.

He finished his drink and thanked Tierney for it. They did not shake hands before he left the pub. Their next meeting may not be so friendly.

***

Driving back to the centre of Newcastle, Cornell thought about his meeting with the godfather of serious crime in the North East. He had the distinct impression Buffalo Bill Tierney was flattered by being asked for information by a DCI. Cornell also wondered what the chief constable would think about him meeting with a known criminal.

As far as he was concerned the meeting had been necessary to confirm he was not barking up the wrong tree with Braithwaite and Whittaker. But something Tierney had said, combined with a local news item nagged at him. He needed to think about it.

***

'Sir,' welcomed David Watkins with an excited look on his face. 'We have some news for you. Good news and bad. Which would you like first?'

Cornell decided to play along with what he considered were rather juvenile requests.

'I'll take the bad news, David,' he said, taking off his anorak and throwing it over the back of a chair.

'Durham police tried to stop a blue Citroen C3 on the A1M this afternoon, but it took off. They gave chase and the Citroen left the motorway on to the A690 towards Durham. It tried to avoid traffic at a roundabout, left the road doing ninety five, rolled over and burst into flames, sir. The road is currently closed.

'The driver?'

'Fried to a cinder, sir. Our boys say it's not a pretty sight. The number plates are false and although the fire is out, it's not yet cool enough to get the chassis number, but we think it must be Janice's car.'

'And the good news?'

'We've found out who owns the craft shop in Herrington, sir.'

'And?'

'Paulmark Developments, sir.'

'Of course it is. A business that is on everyone's minds twenty four seven. I don't even know why we thought it could possibly be anyone else,' said Cornell facetiously. 'David, who the hell is Paulmark bloody Developments?'

'Don't you see, sir? Paul as in Paul Whittaker. Mark as in…'

'Got it. Well done,' Cornell acquiesced. 'What about the upstairs?'

'Owned by the same company. Records show it was transferred from North Tyne Developments seven months ago. Main proprietor of North Tyne

Developments, none other than William Buffalo Bill Tierney.'

'And, sir,' said Sergeant Bob Harvey, replacing his desk phone's receiver, 'Paulmark owns that new brick built house on the road to Rothbury as well.'

Cornell sat down and began to rub his temples.

'Thought you would be pleased, sir,' said Watkins.

'I am. I'm over the bloody moon. I even think, having just come from visiting Buffalo Bill Tierney, which I would be grateful if you kept to yourselves, we have enough evidence now to make arrests,' retorted Cornell.

'So why don't we, sir?' asked Dennison.

'Because we don't yet have our murderer.'

Cornell turned to go to his office.

'Sir,' exclaimed Laura Donaldson, 'I have the Met on the phone wanting to speak to the SIO in the Margaret Whitfield murder.'

She passed the receiver to him.

'DCI Cornell,' he answered.

'Am I speaking to the senior investigating officer in the Margaret Whitfield murder case?'

'Who is this?' demanded Cornell.

'Detective Chief Inspector Brian Turnbull, Metropolitan Police.'

The caller gave his police number, his department and phone extension for Cornell to check against. He racked his memory but couldn't put a face to the name; it had been a long time since he'd worked at Met HQ.

'I'm Max, what can I do for you, Brian?' asked Cornell.

'I've just read about the Margaret Whitfield murder. It was the one-handed strangulation that took my interest.'

'Oh, and why is that?'

'We've had three murders down here, the last one just recently, the other two six months and a year ago, all one-handed strangulations, the left hand, the victims all young escorts.'

'When you put it like that, Brian, do you mean young up-market prostitutes?'

'Yes, Max, if there are such beings.'

'That fits. Any ideas?'

'Our profiler says it's a male, left-handed, tall, probably well over six feet. This is confirmed by forensics although to be honest, I came up with the same description myself.'

'Nothing else, like marriage, accent, schooling, hobbies, job?'

'I take it you are not a fan of profilers, Max.'

'Doesn't sound like you are either, my friend.'

'For what it's worth, Max, I think there's a reason for him only using one hand.'

'I think you are right, else why use only one?' replied Cornell.

Are you near to an arrest?' the Met DCI asked hopefully.

'I think we are near, Brian. Investigations are continuing,' Cornell responded.

'I understand. Will you keep us in the loop?'

'Yes, and I'll start by telling you he's committed another murder since Margaret.'

'Bloody hell. Just in the last few days?'

'Last night.'

'Christ, we've got to catch this guy, Max. Good luck and if you want anything from us, just give us a call.'

Cornell wandered over to the window of the incident room to see if the car which had been following him was parked in view. Daylight was just starting to fade, but he spotted the vehicle.

'Anyone got binoculars?' Cornell hollered.

'Mine are in the car, sir,' said Watkins, 'but Vice have a couple. We often borrow them for surveillance work. They're bloody good ones.'

'Go get me one, will you? Just for a couple of minutes.'

He stood at the window looking at the car. The number plate was in view but too far away to read it with the naked eye. He recalled the vehicle was a VW.

Watkins returned with an Avalon 10 x 42. Good in poor light, Cornell remembered from his Special Branch days.

'See that dark VW over there, David?'

Cornell pointed to the vehicle as Watkins peered through the binoculars.

'The Passat?'

'Yes, what's the number?'

Watkins read out the number and Cornell noted it down.

'Run the plates, David, and thank Vice for the use of their binoculars. I'll be in my office.'

'Hertz Rent-a-Car own the Passat, sir, Newcastle Airport. I'm contacting them for the hirer's name. They usually ask to ring us back, for security.'

'Thanks, David.'

'Sir, what's this got to do with the case?'

'I don't know, David. Probably nothing, but that car has been following me for a few days.'

'Sir,' said David Watkins thirty minutes later, 'the hirer of that vehicle is a white male, James Carter, who produced an American driving licence issued by the District of Columbia. The Hertz person said he was with a woman with an English accent and a tall teenage boy who sounded American. Hired the car last Saturday.'

'Thanks, David. I'm off now. See you tomorrow.'

Cornell collected his coat and left for home to think about the murderer, and who the hell was James Carter?

CHAPTER TWENTY FOUR

Five months ago

Detective Inspector Max Cornell reflected on his police career as he drove east along the M62 on his way from Manchester to Newcastle. He was on his way to an interview with the Northumbria chief constable for a position of detective chief inspector on the murder investigation team, North Tyne.

He was confident. He'd never had a problem with interviews. He never did any research, he just answered questions as best he could. If he was asked a question that had nothing to do with police work and he didn't know the answer, he said so, but would query why was he being asked the question.

After his initial application to join the Metropolitan police, he had never completed another application form. He had been asked to fill one in after obtaining a position with special branch, but he never got around to it and the matter was seemingly forgotten.

Superintendent McNestry had told him about the Newcastle opportunity and Max had said he was interested. He subsequently received a call from the Northumbria chief constable's office requesting he attend for an interview. There was never any mention of an application form and the recruitment process appeared to Cornell to be somewhat unconventional, but he agreed to attend nevertheless.

The chief constable really did want him. His record for bringing down major criminals was outstanding. Since the retirement of her last chief inspector, the vacancy had not been filled. The current acting chief inspector had shown he was not up to the job.

Bringing someone in from another of her commands would weaken that command, so Mary Dewsbury arranged an interview for the apparently awkward Max Cornell.

***

Joining the A1 north, Cornell considered his most important and rewarding case; how his team had followed John Thomas Ramsey relentlessly. How they had set up cameras to watch his activities. How they had left microphones to pick up his conversations and how they had completely missed the woman who followed Ramsey around everywhere.

He had two plain clothes officers in the nightclub the night of the shooting. Both had witnessed the altercation that had taken place between Ramsey and the unfortunate victim, but neither had seen the two men leave the night club to settle their dispute outside.

Ramsey said, when questioned immediately after the murder, that he had been at the toilet when the shooting took place. There was no evidence, CCTV or otherwise, to suggest he hadn't. Then the woman arrived at the police station a day later asking for Max Cornell.

At first, he couldn't believe her testimony. She explained how her son had got a job working for Ramsey but had succumbed to drug taking which had eventually led to his death.

She put the blame for her son's demise firmly on Ramsey who was one of the UK's largest importers and distributers of heroin. She had confronted Ramsey at one of his night clubs, but he'd simply had her thrown out.

So, she set about her own campaign, hoping that somewhere along the line she would catch him red handed distributing drugs. She never thought for one moment that she would catch him committing a murder.

Cornell watched the video on her phone. He asked her to email it to him and when she had checked he had received it, she said she had every faith in him to have Ramsey convicted and then she could have closure for her son.

Ramsey had been arrested for murder later that day and arrived at the police station accompanied by his subordinates and showing his usual bravado.

'Don't worry, Rubenstein will have me out of here in ten minutes,' he said to the increasing number of journalists already waiting outside the police station, all trying to shove recorders and microphones into Ramsey's face.

Ramsey was smiling ear to ear when he was cautioned again for murder and during the desk sergeant's questions relating to his identity.

'Might save time, inspector,' said Rubenstein, Ramsey's lawyer, when they were seated in the interview room, 'if you could just present any physical evidence you have. Anything less than that and we are out of here.'

'Quite right, Mr Rubenstein. I couldn't agree more. How about this for starters?'

Cornell pointed towards the TV screen where his sergeant expertly changed the display from the scene of the four people in the room to the video of the shooting incident.

Ramsey rapidly lost his smile and his colour. Rubenstein, normally loquacious, momentarily lost the ability to speak. Cornell broke the silence.

'I will arrange for you to have a copy of the video, Mr Rubenstein, and allow you time with your client. I assure you of confidentiality while you are receiving his instructions.'

Five minutes later Rubenstein left the interview room and the police station, allowing Ramsey to be taken into custody.

***

From the other side of the desk, the chief constable studied her interviewee and suddenly felt inadequate. Max Cornell was not the least bit nervous. He was almost smiling as he explained about his early career with the Met, special branch and anti-terror and then with the serious crime task force operating in Manchester.

His personnel file, which she had in front of her, was impressive when you considered the higher-than-average arrests, but less so when counting the number of reprimands for not following procedure, or insubordination to senior colleagues.

She challenged him on several issues but he readily came up with an answer each time. Perhaps not with the answer she would have given, or what she had expected, but a coherent answer all the same.

'Have you always broken the rules, inspector?'

'I don't break them, ma'am.'

'Perhaps bending them is more appropriate.'

'I think the word you are looking for, ma'am, is flexibility, much like you interviewing me alone, when there should be a panel of three.'

Chief Constable Dewsbury had not met any senior officer quite like Max Cornell before. Although many ranks below her, he spoke to her as an equal and there were times during the interview when she felt he was the one conducting it.

He was just what she needed.

CHAPTER
TWENTY FIVE

Friday evening

Max Cornell and his foster dog walked down on to the beach at Cullercoats. It was a bright, clear, starry night, almost a full moon, cold, and would probably turn frosty in the early hours.

As soon as they hit the sand Max let Rex off the leash. The dog immediately cocked his leg against the lifeboat station then rapidly headed off towards the shore line to explore.

Max walked off the soft sand on to that which had been compacted by the last tide. He made his way towards the far side of the small beach where Rex, having completed his examination of the remains left by the ebb tide, would meet up with him.

Under the cliff face at the end of the beach Max whistled for the dog and watched it halt its explorations and begin to trot towards his temporary master. Then the big German Shepherd slowed his pace and began to growl, the moonlight highlighting its hackles and reflecting the bared teeth.

'It's alright, Rex,' said Cornell, quickly securing the leash to the dog's collar to avoid any attack and stroking the dog to quieten him down. Cornell turned towards the cliff.

'Hello, Amy.'

Rex, still growling, suddenly barked as a figure emerged from the shadows of the cliff. Max grabbed the dog's collar and gathering his strength, prevented Rex from moving forward.

'How did you know?' asked the woman. She was dressed in jeans, white boots and a thick jacket with a fur trimmed hood lying on her shoulders. She looked the same, possibly a little thinner, as he remembered her from more than a decade ago.

'You've been following me in a car hired to an American. Put two and two together.'

'That's the easy bit. How did you know I was here, on the beach?'

'Hairs on the back of my neck, dog's reaction, plus your hire car is parked just a few yards along from my house. I should ask you how you found me. But what's more important is why?'

'Can we go somewhere? Your house, perhaps, to talk?'

'No. I asked you a question.'

'OK. Your son wants to meet you.'

That stopped Cornell in his tracks. For a second, he struggled to find the words.

'What if I don't want to meet him?'

It was said too quickly and Cornell was not

sure he'd meant it.

'He's your son, Max.'

The dog was quiet now, realising the woman in front of them was not a threat. Cornell allowed Rex to walk forward and smell the woman who reached down and scratched his ears. He liked that.

'You took my son away from me, Amy. Took me a long time to get over that, but I did. I don't want those memories to return.'

'It's taken me two weeks to find you, Max. Tracing you from London, to Manchester, then to here. I'm sorry about your wife, by the way.'

Cornell was about to ask her how she knew, then remembered she had once worked for MI5. She continued, 'I'd rather not have go back to the hotel and tell Todd his real father doesn't want to see him.'

'Why not? I imagine your CIA friend became his father.'

'His stepfather. We got married. I'm Amy Carter now and our son is Todd Carter.'

'So, happy families. Why involve me now?'

'Because, Max, Todd simply wants to meet his real father.'

'Why the hell did you tell him about me?'

'It's not something you should keep from a child. He's known for a long time, but its only recently that he's expressed a wish to meet you. Why would you not want to see your son?'

'Because I learned to live without him. Tell him to drop me a line.'

'Max. Please. Make some time available for him tomorrow.'

'Couldn't, even if I wanted to. I'm right in the middle of a serious investigation. I have no free time at the moment.'

'We go back to the States on Monday, Max.'

'Amy, you left me what? Fifteen, sixteen years ago? You deprived me of my son. No communication since. I got over it. I learned to live without you and him. Don't think you can just come back into my life again on your terms.'

Cornell turned and began to walk away, tugging the dog's leash for it to walk with him. Amy Carter followed.

'You should meet him, Max,' she said to Cornell's back. 'He's grown so tall. He must be over six feet now. Plays basketball and he's very good at....'

Amy Carter paused as she almost walked into Cornell who had stopped and turned around to face her.

'The answer is no, Amy. You have wasted your time.'

She didn't speak. Just stood there on the sand.

Cornell turned and jogged away, letting his dog off the leash again to run in front of him up the hill towards the road and home.

He would not sleep tonight. He would think about his son and why he didn't want to meet him and about a murderer whom he couldn't identify.

CHAPTER TWENTY SIX

Saturday

DC Laura Donaldson was typing away on a laptop. Her desk, covered with notes and statements was directly in view of the whiteboard which she glanced up at from time to time.

She was keying in the information for the cases; putting together all the information and references to evidence for the prostitution and exploitation of prostitution charges in presentable shape for the CPS.

Cornell was not surprised. He had expected Donaldson to be at work when he arrived. He hadn't asked her to do this preparation, she did it because it needed to be done and as she was the best one in the team at doing it, she just did it. He wished she was able to do the same for the murders.

Has she a boy or girl friend? Never speaks of her personal life. Perhaps she doesn't have much of a one. She is always at work anyway.

He, meanwhile, had spent a restless night thinking about his son and why he had no inclination to meet him, then worrying about it as it didn't seem to be natural. He'd finally gone to sleep when he was trying to reconcile his thoughts about the murderer.

***

In view of the speed of build on the Rothbury house and at Cornell's request, Dennison had looked up the identity of the chief planning officer for Northumberland County Council, to find with relief that there were no such initials in either diary.

Dennison was wearing a black and white scarf and a team shirt under his jacket as he was leaving shortly to join the fans coach for Newcastle United's away game with Everton.

David Watkins was trying to make sense of undeleted files IT had retrieved from Paul Whittaker's laptop.

Bob Harvey was trying to secure meetings to obtain arrest and search warrants.

A message had been left for Cornell to contact the lab.

***

Inspector Lambert arrived from Alnwick station where he'd been clearing his admin. The murders had been committed on his patch and Cornell wanted him in Newcastle to assist with planning raids and arrests.

Lambert arrived with a plastic bag of rubbish.

'Shit,' he said. 'I meant to put this in one of the skips out back.'

'What is it?' asked Dennison, putting on his coat, about to leave for the coach to Liverpool. Bob Harvey had asked him if he'd not find it more productive to go on a raid rather than watching the Toon get beat again. Dennison was rendered speechless. Lambert answered his question.

'My wife was complaining about the empty coffee cups and sweet papers in the car,' said Lambert, 'and some leaflets left on the back seat, so I cleaned the car out this morning. I meant to put the crap in the bin at home but got a phone call which distracted me. Then I was going to put it in our skip out back, but forgot.'

A thought occurred to Cornell. He would not call the lab back; he would go in person.

'Here, I'm going to the lab,' said Cornell. 'I'll bin this for you on the way. Back soon.' Cornell picked up the bag of rubbish and left the building, but he didn't put the bag of rubbish in the skip.

***

'I can confirm the person who strangled Sadie Tomkinson was the same person as strangled Margaret Whitfield. Same MO, same DNA.'

Mabel Wainwright showed Cornell the two reports. Then she pointed at another table where there were two plaster casts. 'The shoe tracks are size twelve, which is the size I would expect our murderer to be. Any idea who it is yet?'

Instead of answering, Cornell produced Lambert's plastic bag of rubbish.

'Any chance of a quick DNA test on the coffee cups in this lot? It's urgent.'

'Tom can do it. Tom,' she called out to her assistant, 'do a DNA on this, would you? Push it through if you would for the good chief inspector.'

'Marian arrive back home alright?' Cornell asked.

'Yes, Marian is home and looking forward to meeting you.'

'Why? What have you told her?'

'That you are funny and clever and a nice, reliable person with impeccable manners.'

'And what did she say to that?'

'She asked when we were getting married.'

Cornell felt himself blush, but appreciated the humour.

Wainwright saw his anxiety. 'Don't worry, Max. My daughter is also funny and too clever for her own good sometimes. Nice most of the time, but not very reliable and no manners at all.'

'Should I be looking forward to meeting her, or not?'

'I think the two of you will get on fine, but you are coming for lunch tomorrow, or aren't you?'

'I'm really trying to make it, Mabel. If I do, can I bring my dog?'

'Dog? What dog? You don't have a dog, do you?'

Cornell explained the death of his neighbour and his acquisition, if only temporary, of a dog. 'Well, if it's tiny and not going to defecate all over my home, I suppose so.'

'Well, it's house trained and not the biggest dog in the world.'

'In that case, your dog will be very welcome.'

'Chief inspector,' said Tom Mawson who was at another table removing the contents of the rubbish bag Cornell had brought in. 'Do you want this leaflet tested as well?"

'What leaflet?' Cornell asked.

'This,' Mawson showed him a leaflet which he held with tweezers in a gloved hand.

Cornell read some of the first paragraph then suddenly smiled broadly.

'You asked if I had any idea who the murderer is, Mabel.'

'Do you?' she answered.

'Ninety nine point nine percent. The DNA from those coffee cups will confirm it.'

Cornell left the lab in haste without any goodbyes.

'Was it something I said?' asked Tom Mawson after the door closed.

Cornell almost ran back to the station. He knew who the murderer was. It was someone he had never met, nor spoken to and but for a discarded piece of paper, may well have escaped the arms of Northumbria police.

***

'Got them, sir,' said Sergeant Bob Harvey waving warrants as he entered the incident room. 'When are we serving them?'

'As soon as we have planned who does what. How many uniforms have you got on standby, Shaun?'

'Thirty, sir,' replied Lambert. 'Some of them not happy about missing the match.'

'Since when did football come before protecting the public? Anyway, it's an away match,' said Cornell.

'Yes, but it's on the tele in the "Iron Foundry."'

'They can watch the highlights if there are any, on Match of the Day,' admonished Cornell.

'What about the murderer, sir?' asked David Watkin. 'The arrests will alert him, won't they?'

'Don't worry, David. DC Donaldson and I will be arresting the murderer at the same time as you are conducting the raids. So leave me some uniforms, Bob.'

Everyone stopped what they were doing. Conversation ended. All eyes centred on Cornell; DC Donaldson as surprised as anyone.

'Err...are you going to tell us who it is, chief inspector?' asked Bob Harvey after a lengthy pause.

'No, not yet. I will advise Laura on the way to the arrest. It's not that I don't trust you all, I do, but I want you to concentrate on your arrests, not mine. Oh, and I want you all in tomorrow morning to conduct interviews.'

There was silence in the incident room as Cornell moved to his office, leaving his team feeling rather let down.

Sergeant Harvey broke the tension.

'Alright everyone, listen up. There is a reason why the boss won't disclose the name to us at the moment and like he said, we need to concentrate on our jobs. So, instead of discussing it, we will have a sweep. The usual five pound entrance fee. Write the name of who you think the murderer is and put your answer in the sweep box.'

From out of a cupboard, Harvey removed a cardboard box. It had a slot in the top in which to post entries. It was used for Grand Nationals, Derby's, World Cups, FA Cup Finals and most other national and international competitive occurrences.

It was open to all departments and as the murders were still headline news, the box would be circulated amongst them later in the day. Entries would still be made although no one outside of MIT would have a chance of winning, but half the entrance fee went to charity.

CHAPTER TWENTY SEVEN

Four months ago

After leaving his job interview with the chief constable, Max Cornell drove along the south banks of the Tyne towards Ryton. It was the town where he had been brought up and was where his mother had returned to after his father had died. Cornell had not informed his mother he would call as he knew the effort she would make to welcome him home.

He had an arm's length relationship with his mother. They had never fallen out but he had not visited her, and vice versa, for a number of years. Bi-monthly telephone calls had sufficed for them to continue their association. Nor was she aware that he was in line for a transfer to Newcastle with a promotion.

On arriving at her home, he opened the gate and was immediately impressed with the garden. Lawns mowed and tidy flower beds; his mother had always been a keen gardener.

He strolled up the path towards the front

door and rang the bell. When it opened, his mother stood silhouetted against a background light holding the door with one hand and carrying a miniature dachshund in the other.

'Hello, son. Coffee?'

***

'Do you think you'll get the job, then?' asked his mother after they had finished the meal she had hastily conjured up from the varying contents of her fridge.

'I think I've already got it.'

'You always were so confident, Max. How do you think you've got it?'

'The chief constable's body language, and she let slip one time saying "when" not "if."'

'And you can tell from that?'

'Yeah. You pick it up from interviewing villains. They think you don't know when they are lying.'

'Not sure I would like your job, Max, but you have done well for yourself. It's a pity you don't have someone to share it with.'

Here we go again.

'Haven't made a great success of relationships, Mother.'

'You shouldn't let what Amy did and what happened to Michelle stop you from having happiness in another relationship.'

'Happy the way I am,' he lied. 'Anyway, what's with the dog?' he said, nimbly changing the subject, while looking down at the little dog sitting quietly by the side of the table, hoping someone would give it a tasty morsel.

'Her name is Annie. She's my soul mate and she understands English. Don't you girl?'

The little dog stood and wagged its tail furiously, expecting the attention to be accompanied with food, only to be disappointed, receiving light taps on its rear end instead.

'She won't need much exercise, that's a fact,' stated Cornell.

'You'd be surprised. I take her out twice a day and she helps me in the garden.'

'Your garden is lovely, Mother. Do you do it all yourself?'

'Of course not. I have a gardener comes in twice a week. Which leads me to ask, where are you going to live if you get this job? You are not thinking of crashing in on me, I hope.'

'No, I'll find somewhere in Newcastle, I expect.'

'How about Cullercoats?'

'Cullercoats,' exclaimed Cornell. 'Why on earth would I think of Cullercoats?'

'I own a house there. I let it out during the summer.'

'Never thought of you as a property tycoon, Mother.'

'Well, I am. I have another house in Wooler, up north and I'm looking at another at Embleton.'

'What made you buy houses, Mother? I

assume you have bought them.'

'Quite simply, Max, I have too much money. I have an army pension, a teacher's pension and an old age pension and a tidy sum in the bank, but it's made no interest since the financial crash of 2008. So, I invest in property. I took out mortgages and what I earn from rentals pays them off and more.'

'Is the house in Cullercoats available then?'

'It will be in two weeks' time. I have some bookings for next year but I can divert them to other holiday lets in the area. It will only take a few phone calls.'

'Right, then. I'll take it.'

'Excellent. It will be seven hundred and fifty a month and you will pay for your own gas, electricity and water. I pay the council tax. There is no landline. Agreed?'

Cornell nodded. He had forgotten how governmental his mother was. He had no choice but to accept.

CHAPTER TWENTY EIGHT

Saturday afternoon

Detective Chief Inspector Max Cornell and Detective Constable Laura Donaldson left the police station on a cool, clear afternoon, darkness only just beginning to descend.

They were en route to arrest the murderer of Margaret Whitfield and Sadie Tomkinson.

They used Cornell's car and he drove them out of the police station car park and headed west. Two squad cars filled with four uniformed constables in each and a custody van followed them.

Laura Donaldson was enthused. She knew the initials of the murderer but had no idea of his identity and was eager to hear the name from her superior.

At the same time as this convoy set out, four teams had been selected and sent on separate operations. One under the leadership of Inspector Shaun Lambert had been sent to raid the Rothbury house. Another, under Sergeant Bob Harvey to raid the Herrington Harbour craft shop and whatever was going on upstairs.

Two uniformed sergeants from other commands were co-opted in to arrest Paul Whittaker and Mark Braithwaite.

'Are you going to tell me who it is, sir?' asked Laura Donaldson finally.

'It is someone who doesn't live in this area, Laura. He arrived here on the afternoon of Saturday 5th January having already pre-arranged his entertainment for the Saturday and Sunday nights, that entertainment being Janice. She put his initials in her diary, but until this morning they meant absolutely nothing to me.'

The three car convoy took to the West Road out of the centre of Newcastle, turned right on to the A1 and headed north for the Ponteland exit. Only a few miles now to the airport where the arrest would take place. Cornell had made arrangements for his fleet of vehicles to drive through the barriers and park off to one side of the terminal.

'I still can't work it out,' said Donaldson.

Cornell told her the name of the murderer.

'Do you want to do the honours, Laura?'

'Yes, sir, I would like that. I'll do it on behalf of the girls.'

They walked into Departures and towards the British Airways check-in, Donaldson still shocked at learning the perpetrator's name.

There was a short queue, the subject of the

arrest had not yet arrived. The uniformed police were asked to stay in the background and only come forward when the arrest was being made.

After only a few minutes their perpetrator, standing head and shoulders above his entourage which included two bodyguards, entered through the main doors of the airport and headed for the BA check-in.

At the self-service machine, Cornell and Donaldson stepped forward, their ID's attached to their lapels. The uniformed officers came forward and stood around them.

'Jeremy Symonds, I am Detective Constable Laura Donaldson. I am arresting you for the murders of Margaret Whitfield and Sadie Tomkinson. You do not have to say anything, but it may harm…….'

***

'I would never have believed it was him. An MP! Christ, I've been alone with him in my car. How did you know it was Symonds, sir?' asked Inspector Shaun Lambert later in the day when all of the day's operations had been completed.

'Since Margaret Whitfield's murder, we've known the killer was very tall. We also knew he had used only his left hand to strangle his victims, but we didn't know why. Fairly useless clues. We had his DNA, but he's not on the database. We discovered his initials, but who would associate them with a MP who doesn't live in the area? Then he kills Sadie Tomkinson and leaves his footprints, but whose do we match them up with? Then the Met ring me about their unsolved cases involving strangulation with just one hand, the left. Surely the same perpetrator. Tierney told me to cast the net wider than the local area and within minutes I see Symonds on his television: a very tall man not from these parts and wearing gloves. It did make me wonder at the time if he could be our man, but that's all I could do. Wonder.

'Then you brought in the rubbish from your car, Shaun. I could see there were two disposable coffee cups and I remembered you telling me you were taking Symonds to Berwick. The lab wanted to speak to me so I decided on a whim, to take the rubbish bag across in person. It was a bonus to discover a crumpled publicity leaflet describing Symonds as six foot six with a false arm. That's why he wore gloves, to disguise the fact, and that's also why he only used his left hand to strangle. He couldn't use his right.'

'I just never realised,' said Lambert who had been shaking his head almost continuously since learning the murderer's identity. 'Every time I was with him, he wore gloves. I thought that despite his size, he was really suffering from the cold.'

'Apparently,' interjected Donaldson who had Symonds web site loaded on her laptop, 'according to his publicity, he keeps his false arm down by his side most of the time, because he doesn't like to advertise the fact it's false and he's sick of having to explain how he lost the original one.'

'How did he lose it?' asked Watkins.

'Car accident fifteen years ago when he was at university,' replied Donaldson.

'But should we not have waited until we got the DNA from Inspector Lambert's cups before arresting Symonds?' asked Watkins.

'Two things, David. One, his shoes are the same size and the same tread as the casts taken at South Shields, which was enough to bring him in for questioning, and two, if he had got on that plane, we may have lost him.'

'But he's an MP, how could he have gone underground?'

'David, when you've got a minute, read up about an MP called John Stonehouse. He tried to disappear in the seventies to avoid arrest for serious fraud and had he been a bit cleverer, may well have achieved it. Also, I wanted Symonds here, in our nick, not arguing for weeks with the Met about jurisdiction of where he should be processed.'

'What about the minders, sir?' asked Laura Donaldson.

'They were employees, presumably of Paulmark Developments, Laura, although I doubt if they received pay slips or paid due taxes. Unless any of the girls come forward and press criminal charges, we don't actually have anything on them.'

Plans were drawn up for interviews to take place the following morning and as most of the cells in the station were now occupied as a result of the raids, alternative accommodation was arranged elsewhere for Newcastle's Saturday night party set.

***

Cornell rang his chief constable at her home to advise her of the successful arrests and to arrange for the interviewing of Braithwaite.

'You've done what, chief inspector?' exclaimed Chief Constable Mary Dewsbury who was at home. 'I could have sworn you just said you had arrested an MP for murder.'

'You heard right, ma'am. The Honourable Jeremy Symonds.'

'My God, Max! I hope you are right. You've got his DNA, haven't you?'

'Should have it tomorrow or Monday, ma'am.'

'What! Oh my God.'

'Tomorrow or Monday, ma'am,' Cornell repeated.

'You mean you have arrested a Member of Parliament, a minister not least, for murder, without waiting for DNA results? My God, Max, what evidence have you got?'

'The man looks big and strong enough to have committed the murders. He's a Londoner who may have committed similar crimes in the big city. His initials were in Janice's diary for that weekend. The shoe casts made of the footprints found at the murder scene at South Shields match his size, and size twelve is not that common, ma'am.'

'I just wish you had waited for the DNA results, Max, to be absolutely sure.'

'Didn't want him to get on that aircraft, ma'am. We could have lost him to bureaucracy and I needed to arrest him before you suspended Braithwaite.'

'I hope you are right, Max, or you and I will be partners driving around in a patrol car as of Monday.'

'Oh, that's not so bad, ma'am,' said Cornell ending the call.

***

The custody sergeant opened Jeremy Symonds' cell door to allow Cornell entry. Symonds was sitting on the platform that served as a bed, his left arm curled around his knees, his uncoupled prosthetic right arm beside him.

He was wearing an orangey red custody suit, his clothes taken away for analysis. Forensics would be busy tonight. Symonds had declined a duty solicitor in favour of his own who was on his way to the police station.

'I'm Detective Chief Inspector Max Cornell, senior investigator into the murders of Margaret Whitfield and Sadie Tomkinson.'

'Come to gloat, have you?'

'No, just thought I'd pop in and ask you why

you thought you could get away with murdering two young girls?'

'You've got that to prove, chief inspector.'

'You tried to get rough with Janice and Margaret, didn't you? And they didn't like it. Janice got away, but Margaret didn't, did she? Then Sadie was going to tell all and when you found out, you had to shut her up too. Couldn't let your reputation be tarnished, could you?'

'So, prove it.'

'Mr Symonds, I only arrest people when I can prove it. I also know you've been a naughty boy in London before this. Let's put it this way, Mr Symonds; I don't think it likely you will be asking the prime minister any more questions on a Wednesday lunch time.'

After closing Symonds cell door, the duty sergeant opened Mark Braithwaite's. He was lying down on the bench, hands behind his head, his chin blacker than Cornell had ever seen it.

'No need for you to get up, Mr Braithwaite. They treating you alright down here?'

'Piss off.'

'Now that's not very nice, Mr Braithwaite. I guess you are thinking about your future? Might be in your interest to come clean, don't you think? Close the door, sergeant.'

Paul Whittaker was standing at the rear of his cell when his door was opened. He immediately started off with a soliloquy.

'Don't you know who I am? I am Paul Silas Whittaker, QC. Did you know that? I am a barrister with an excellent reputation. I have influence in this city. Do you know who I am? I am Paul Silas Whittaker….'

Cornell shook his head then gestured for the sergeant to close the cell door.

'He sounds quite mad, sir,' indicated the sergeant.

'I wouldn't disagree, sergeant,' answered Cornell, who had noticed Whittaker's bright but unfocused eyes. 'You on all night?'

'Yes, sir, and I will look after him,' replied the sergeant, anticipating Cornell's next question.

The next cell contained three punters, all well-known personalities of one form or another. Two were discovered during the raid on the craft shop in Herrington and the other at the Rothbury house.

Cornell stood in the doorway while his prisoners, two seated and one standing, looked at him with worried expressions.

'You are famous people,' said Cornell, 'paying four figure sums of money for nights of entertainment with girls who are little more than children. Imagine how that will go down with your public. Because the girls were threatened with harm if they left the business or reported what they were involved in, we are treating it as them being forced to provide sexual services, which is a crime. We will be putting our cases against you to the CPS tomorrow. If you manage to get decent solicitors, you might get bail. You should use the time between then and your court cases to contact your agents regarding upcoming engagements.'

***

At seven o'clock, Cornell recorded a short news bulletin which would be aired on the next local TV news slot. It announced the arrest and the name of the suspected murderer of Margaret Whitfield and Sadie Tomkinson. Also announced was the discovery of a sex ring owned by high profile figures from the North East. Their arrests, alongside those of a number of their clients, had also been made. However, their names would not be released until midday tomorrow after further investigations and interviews had been undertaken.

***

Before he left the station at seven thirty, Cornell rang Mabel Wainwright at home.

'I know,' she said, 'there is no way you can make tomorrow lunch time. I've just got in from work myself. Your office has created a considerable amount of work, Max.'

'Good for business though, Mabel.'

'I know, but I'm trying to get to know what my daughter has been up to in the States and I keep getting interrupted. Now, even I couldn't make tomorrow lunch time, so how about tomorrow night? You must be free by then. I can change lunch into dinner.'

'You are determined, aren't you?'

'You are so right.'

'OK, say eight o'clock.'

***

It was almost nine when he arrived home that night. He locked his car door and looked up at the houses. Rex was being looked after by Jenny Laidlaw.

The dog was at her window looking out and Cornell could see that it was barking with excitement when he was spotted. Mrs Laidlaw appeared at the window, then took the dog to the front door letting him go as Cornell walked up the path.

The dog ran at Cornell excitedly.

'He's been very good,' Jenny said, 'but he's been at the window looking out for you most of the day.'

'Thanks for looking after him, Jenny.'

'Oh, I don't mind. He's good to talk to. If only he could talk back. I think he understands what I'm saying.'

'Come on lad, get your leash.'

The dog went to Jenny Laidlaw who held the leash out for the dog. He gently took it from her and returned with it to Cornell.

It was another cold, clear, starry night with

almost a full moon. A torch was unnecessary on the beach. The big German Shepherd easily saw the ball thrown by Cornell, and hurtled after it.

It gave Cornell the time to think about his son and the arrests. His son, he was surprised about, but he felt no feeling of love or even affiliation towards him. That concerned him.

Turning his thoughts to work; Braithwaite and Whittaker would go down. Whittaker, he was sure would end up in some kind of mental institution, or whatever they were called these days. Braithwaite, a long spell of solitary awaited him. being a high-ranking police officer.

Their clients would be charged but they would have the top legal minds defending them and would probably get off, unless the girls got together and took civil actions against them.

The minders would probably not be prosecuted, unless any of the girls pointed the finger of violence.

Jeremy Symonds MP, depending on how he pleads, would get twenty to thirty years, his downfall triggering a by-election. The opposition would be rubbing their hands.

Cornell returned from the beach to the rear entrance of his home. He unlocked his back door and ushered the dog in, but it immediately went to the front door and started growling. Cornell refrained from putting on the lights, instead he walked quietly into his front room so he could see what or who was at his door.

Three people stood on his pathway, illuminated by a street light. The nearest to the house was Amy, another, between her and the gate was a hulk of a boy and a third, a male standing at the gate, whom, judging by his body language did not want to be there.

The dog rushed into the sitting room and Cornell grabbed him. If Rex saw the people outside, he would start barking. Whispering to the dog and stroking his head Max managed to keep him quiet and restrain him from standing on his hind legs to see out of the window.

Cornell knew he couldn't be seen in the darkness. He also knew he should open the door to greet his son after all these years, but something held him back.

He looked out at the face of the large youth. The boy was chewing gum, a practice Cornell detested, and he drank from a can of Red Bull.

Cornell felt no fondness, no attraction, no love, no compunction to open the front door and throw his arms around his son. The youth looked nothing like him and Cornell couldn't remember anyone in his family being that big. He lip read the boy who said he wanted to leave and that they were wasting time here.

Amy was trying to persuade him and his step- father otherwise, but the two males were having none of it.

The trio eventually walked away, but not before the boy placed the empty Red Bull can on

Cornell's gatepost.

The cheeky bugger.

The VW Passat eventually drove off and Cornell let the dog go. He put his front paws on the window sill and was about to bark when he realised there was nothing to bark at. Instead, he ran to the front door and Cornell followed, letting him out into the garden. Amy had graciously closed the gate as she left.

Cornell went to his kitchen and collected a freezer bag. As he did so, he reflected on what he'd just witnessed, struggling to believe the boy was his son and whether the son really wanted to meet his father. Was there something else the son and his parents wanted?

Cornell went outside and collected the Red Bull can and placed it inside the freezer bag.

CHAPTER TWENTY NINE

Sunday

Cornell arose at seven and got dressed. He would take Rex out before heading off to work. A busy day loomed.

On his return from the beach, there were some people at Mrs Nic's house. Her relatives, assumed Cornell. Come to take the dog no doubt, which saddened him. In just a couple of days he had become completely attached to the big German Shepherd.

He considered absconding, but his car was parked outside his house. He gritted his teeth as Ernie Nicholson, who stood smoking a cigarette at the gate, introduced himself.

'I'm the next-door neighbour,' Cornell said. 'I was looking after your mother's dog until you came for him.'

'Thanks, mate. Can you take him? We don't want him and we live in a flat. No dogs allowed.'

'What about other relatives?' asked Cornell, his hopes rising slightly.

'Well, I have a sister who lives abroad and an elder brother who is in jail at the moment, so, you can have him if you want him.'

A lady appeared at the door.

'Are you the man who lives next door?' she asked.

'Yes. It appears I could be the dog's new owner,' answered Cornell.

'That's so good of you. We are clearing out Ernie's mother's things and I found these.'

She produced the bill of sale for Rex as a puppy; a pedigree document and vets bills.

'That's great,' said Cornell. 'Can you write, "sold to Max Cornell," and today's date on the bill of sale and sign it please?'

'Sure.'

And Max became the legal owner of Rex.

He decided he would take the dog to work today. He was well behaved and it didn't look good acquiring a dog then leaving it at home or with a neighbour.

***

Cornell took Rex to his office and after all the team and others had stroked it, he told it to lie down, which it duly did.

'Sir,' said Laura Donaldson, 'three girls have rung in saying they saw the news last night and want to make statements against Braithwaite and Whittaker.'

'But we haven't released their names yet.'

'All the more evidence for us, sir. They were pretty explicit as to who was behind this sex ring you talked about on last night's bulletin and their arrests have given the girls confidence.'

'OK. Document it.'

'Sir, two of the girls asked about the minders. Some of them didn't treat the girls well. One in particular, the one called Kurt.'

'Get them to come in and make statements. We'll take it from there.'

His phone rang.

'Good morning, Max,' said Mabel Wainwright. 'I've come into the lab this morning to help with the backlog created by your lot.'

'Good morning, Mabel. I trust that will not interfere with your meal preparations for this evening?'

'I'm leaving at two to attend to that, but the reason for my ringing this morning is to tell you we have the DNA results from those coffee cups.'

'Great. Your next sentence will determine whether I remain in post or commence driving a patrol car partnering the ex-chief constable as of Monday morning.'

'One match was of Inspector Lambert; the other is a match for the DNA we found on Margaret Whitfield and Sadie Tomkinson. How did you know that, Max? I'm also sending Tom Mawson over to you to take prints of Symonds left hand, to compare with the marks arounds the girls' throats.'

'Good idea. The more shit I can throw at the bastard, the more will stick.'

'Quite. And the DNA from the body retrieved from the car that caught fire at Durham was on the database. A Kurt Gruber. Know him?'

'Yes, he was the chief minder, I think.'

'See you tonight, chief inspector, or is it acting superintendent?'

He was about to answer, but she closed the call. He hadn't thought about that.

Cornell opened his office door and walked into the main area of the incident room.

'We've got him! DNA's a match,' he declared to his team and others.

Everyone applauded. 'Who won the sweep?' asked Cornell above the applause.

'No one, sir,' answered David Watkins. 'We did get some interesting answers though. Your dog was one.'

'That dog has never hurt a soul in its whole life,' exclaimed Cornell. 'What happens to the winnings now?'

'Half goes to charity, sir, the balance is held over for the next sweep,' answered Bob Harvey.

'Will I be able to participate in that?'

'Hopefully, sir. Dennison thought you should have been asked to partake in this one.'

Cornell returned to his office shaking his head, undecided whether Harvey was telling the truth or making a joke.

***

Sergeant Bob Harvey switched on the tape and gave the names of all those present. It was of no surprise to Cornell that Symonds' solicitor was the Noble Lord Sir Anthony Bedwell-Sloan, having just arrived from his estate outside Hexham.

'I have instructed my client to answer, "no comment" to every question, chief inspector,' said the solicitor.

'That's all right,' responded Cornell. 'However, in view of that bit in the caution that states, "it may harm your defence if you do not answer when questioned," I am going to ask you a bucket load of questions. So, I hope neither of you have anything planned for lunch.'

And so, the one-way interview continued for the next three hours. That should impress the chief constable thought Cornell as he left interview room two.

***

Chief Constable Mary Dewsbury came into the incident room having interviewed ex Chief Superintendent Mark Braithwaite. She asked for quiet.

'First of all, I would like to thank you for all the hard work you have put in on this extremely difficult case, or should I say cases.'

Cornell, tired from his interview with Symonds, switched off for the accolade. He hated praise, often given when it wasn't appropriate.

But his ears pricked up when the chief constable finished her appreciations and started to relate her interview with Braithwaite.

'I'm pleased to say that Mark Braithwaite has made a statement admitting the offence of jointly owning and running a brothel, or brothels, for the purpose of prostitution. He will plead guilty and will co-operate fully with us, hoping doing so will lessen his sentence. As a result, he has implicated Paul Whittaker as his partner and also given me information regarding Janice Whittaker.

'Braithwaite obtained this information from a minder stroke bodyguard called Kurt who was at the Herrington building on the Saturday night but subsequently disappeared. There was an altercation between Symonds and Janice shortly after the two were introduced, resulting in Janice leaving the building and running away. It was another minder who ran after her but neither had returned to the building by the time Symonds left. Braithwaite thinks the minder either murdered Janice or watched her drown, then did a runner, as it were.

'Symonds therefore, couldn't have known Janice was dead when he left the Herrington building early on the Sunday morning to return to his hotel in Alnwick. He was in an extremely agitated state, however, having paid an exorbitant fee for services he had not received. He demanded another girl for the Sunday night and arrangements were made for him to meet Margaret Whitfield at the Rothbury house.'

'So, we may never know what happened to Janice, ma'am, unless we can track this minder down,' stated Bob Harvey.

'That's right, Sergeant Harvey,' continued the chief constable. 'Braithwaite says apart from Kurt, who was the chief minder, he doesn't know the minders' names. That side of the business was left to Whittaker,' said the chief constable.

'We have found some names on Whittaker's laptop, ma'am. Could refer to them, I suppose,' said Watkins.

'As far as Whittaker himself is concerned,' said Harvey, 'I'm not sure how much sensible information we'll get from him. I think involving his daughter in prostitution made him a bit mad, if he wasn't already, but being caught and arrested has sent him over the edge, ma'am, just like his wife. Bedwell-Sloan doesn't want anything to do with him and Whittaker refuses to see the duty solicitor, asking for us to contact celebrated solicitors in London, most of whom are retired and some are dead.'

'Oh dear,' she exclaimed. 'Max, how did your interview with Symonds go?'

'It was a "no comment" affair, ma'am, but I went through the evidence with him anyway. Bedwell-Sloan was very quiet after I'd told him Janice had put his client's initials in her diary as her escort for the Saturday night. Went totally mute when I mentioned Symonds has form in London, and the Met are closing in on him. Then I mentioned his shoes, which have now been checked and the treads are identical to the casts taken at South Shields. The sand found in his shoes is of the same content as the South Shields beach. Although some of the evidence is circumstantial, he's going to be hard pressed to argue the DNA.'

'Good! Good! I notice the press are outside, so I think it's only right that we invite them in to the conference room. Max, with me.'

After the chief constable had explained the crimes and the arrests to the throng of journalists, she brought Cornell forward to answer questions.

'Was Janice Whittaker murdered, chief inspector?' asked a female reporter sitting at the front.

'I don't know. I know she drowned and I know she ran from violence to the place of her death. But whether she jumped or was pushed, I don't think we will ever know. '

To another question he answered, 'We found Margaret's car in Whittaker's garage. I suspect it was driven there from Rothbury on the Monday morning after her death, but we don't know for certain. In the grand old scheme of things, it's not important.'

Then he was asked if anything positive had come out of the deaths. Strange question, he thought, but some modern-day reporters take a philosophy degree.

'Does anything positive ever come out of any death?' answered Cornell. 'I suppose we could say the investigation into Janice's death, rather than label it as a suicide, was positive as it led us to discovering a rather nasty sex ring.'

'Chief Inspector,' called out a wild haired reporter sitting off to one side. By his attitude Cornell immediately sensed trouble. 'Jed Temperly, The Chronicle. Can you explain why you were seen associating with a known criminal, Buffalo Bill Tierney, on Friday?'

Someone, probably one of Tierney's lot had leaked.

'Yes, Mr Temperly, I was doing my job. I meet with people of all persuasions, all the time. It's what I do.'

'You were seen accepting a drink from him.'

'So what? Do you think he was bribing me with a pint of John Smith's? I think you need to get out more, Mr Temperly. No more questions.'

'Why were you associating with a known criminal on Friday, Max?' asked the chief constable as they were climbing the stairs back to the incident room.

'Just doing my job, ma'am. Like I said.'

'I don't know whether I should keep my distance from your investigations, Max, or closely monitor them. But watch Temperly, though. He's a trouble maker. So, what are you doing about Whittaker?'

'I'm not about to interview him, ma'am.

I don't think I would get anything sensible out of him. Instead, I'm arranging a psychiatric assessment. I suspect he's looking at spending the rest of his life in some kind of institution.'

DC Laura Donaldson entered the room as Cornell was talking.

'Nothing more than he deserves,' she said. 'Drove his wife to drink and turned his daughter into a prostitute. I don't think there will be many protesters outside the court clamouring for his release.'

'Laura,' said Bob Harvey, 'that's not like you.'

Donaldson did not respond, instead pointed at Cornell's office where, through the glass partition, three people could be seen.

'It's Mr and Mrs Harris, sir, and Edith Whittaker,' said Laura Donaldson. 'They came to see you about Janice. You were tied up with the press conference, so I put them in your office. Hope that was OK.'

'Thanks, Laura,' answered Cornell.

Edith stood up as Cornell entered the office, as did his dog.

'Hello again, Edith. Please sit down. I see you've made a friend of my dog.' Cornell acknowledged Mr and Mrs Harris with a nod.

'I want to apologise, Mr Cornell,' declared Edith.

'What for, Edith?'

'I should have told you about Janice. I knew she was a sex worker.'

'Yes, you should, but as it turned out, it didn't make much difference. Did she ask you to join her?'

'No, just the opposite. Janice told me she wanted to get away from the business, but she was being watched and she was frightened. I said that was her fault for going into that business in the first place. I feel guilty now. If I'd been a bit more friendly towards her, she might still be alive. I called her names and told her I didn't want to see her again.' At which point Edith started to cry. Her grandmother gave her a tissue. After wiping her eyes and blowing her nose, Edith continued between sobs. 'When I think back, she was crying out for help but I was so sickened by what she was doing, I couldn't see it.'

'What Janice got into was not your fault, Edith. When did you tell your grandmother what you knew?'

'How did you know that I did?' she sobbed.

'I'm a detective.'

'She told us last night, chief inspector,' said Mrs Harris, 'after we had watched your news bulletin. I told her she had to come here and apologise to you, as it might have made your investigations easier and quicker if she'd told you what she knew.'

'I didn't realise it at the time. I'm so sorry,' said Edith, no longer weeping.

'I don't think we will need you as a witness for the trials, Edith, but thank you for coming in today.'

Edith Whittaker looked anxiously at her grandfather.

'Edith wants to join the police force when she finishes her education, chief inspector,' said Mr Harris. 'This won't affect her doing that, will it?'

Cornell smiled, suddenly realising the real reason why the Harris's had attended the station.

'No, Mr Harris. Edith will not be charged with any offence, so she will have no record.'

***

A satisfied Max Cornell and his dog left the police station late afternoon. The last official action of his day had been to arrange a meeting with the acting CPS lead prosecutor for the following morning.

Prior to that, he'd had a can of beer with his team in the incident room to celebrate the successful arrests but left soon after to allow them to continue the celebrations without him. He would go home, have a shower and make his way to the home of Mabel Wainwright for dinner and to meet her daughter.

***

He was ten minutes late when he and Rex arrived at Mabel Wainwright's door. He'd brought a bottle of decent red wine and flowers as an apology. He should be looking forward to the company but being unused to it, he was seriously anxious. He could turn around and walk away, but decided to risk it.

He rang the doorbell of the detached house and stood waiting with Rex, who he kept leashed. The dog sat down as instructed, his ears pricked high in anticipation of who would answer the door. After a few moments, an outside light above them flashed on and the door opened. Rex stood up and took a step forward.

'Oh! My God,' said a shocked Mabel Wainwright, holding her hand across her heart while looking down at the big German Shepherd. 'It's a bloody wolf! Does it bite?'

'Of course.'

'Please come in before a neighbour sees it and calls the zoo,' she replied, standing behind the door to protect herself. 'I expect I'll have to move some of the furniture.'

Cornell entered the hall and glanced at his host. He couldn't believe the transformation she had made from a working Mabel to a leisurely Mabel. She had gone to some lengths to make herself look beautiful and had succeeded.

He handed her the flowers and the wine, then looked down at the Red Bull can in the freezer bag.

'This isn't a present,' he said.

'I'm not too disappointed,' she responded with a questionable look.

'This isn't work, Mabel, but I would be very grateful if you could check out the DNA on this can. I'll pay if I have to.'

'Oh! I am intrigued. I think I can allow a freebee now and then. Hang your coat up in that cupboard.' She pointed to a small doorway at the bottom of the stairs. 'Leave the can in there on the floor. Then do come in, Marian will be wondering what we are up to.'

Cornell shrugged out of his anorak, hung it up, then followed Rex who was straining at the leash, eager to see beyond the doorway.

'Max, this is my daughter, Marian. Marian this is Max and his dog. I'll just put these flowers in water,' Mabel said whilst leaving the room.

A pretty girl, dark haired and slim, of around sixteen or seventeen arose from a chair putting down a magazine which she probably had not been reading. Almost as tall as her mother and while not a close resemblance, you could identify they were mother and daughter despite different hair colours.

'Oh! What a lovely dog,' she said.

Max unleashed Rex who walked forward and sat down obediently in front of Marian. He wasn't stupid, he loved being scratched and stroked around the ears.

'So pleased to meet you, Max. Mother was really worried you weren't going to make it. Do I call you Max?'

'Max will do fine. And I'm pleased to meet you too, Marian,' Cornell responded.

'Marian, I need some help in here,' shouted

Mabel from the kitchen. 'Max, what do I give your dog? I'm right out of antelope haunches.'

Max Cornell smiled. He was going to enjoy the evening after all.

ABOUT THE AUTHOR

Douglas John Knox

Douglas John Knox is best known for his action packed mystery thrillers, including the DCI Max Cornell series. Mostly set in the North East of England, but his tales can take you off to the capital and overseas.

Although blessed with a colourful imagination, Douglas didn't start writing fiction until he retired from the Civil Service in 2005. It was then, with a compulsion to record his creations, instead of just dreaming them, that he was stimulated to write.

Once a resident of County Durham, Douglas John Knox now lives in North Northumberland, the setting for many of his novels.

When not writing, Douglas enjoys fly fishing and tying his own flies, gardening, which includes tending a large allotment and painting, both in watercolours and oils.

Also known to have the occasional glass of red wine.

BOOKS BY THIS AUTHOR

At Rest At Last

Tells the story of a young wife who loses her life in a road traffic accident in a remote village in North Northumberland to a hit and run vehicle. The car and its occupants are later identified but the police are only able to bring minor traffic charges against them. The husband does not believe his dead wife will ever be at rest until justice is properly served. From the family farm in Northumberland to the deserts of Iraq, and over a period of twenty-five years, all occupants of the vehicle are traced by the husband who delivers his own kind of judgement. A police officer and distant relative whose advances were rejected by the wife before she was married, is driven to gather evidence against the husband to settle family scores and satisfy his ego.

Death Factory

Involves a solicitor who takes on the might of

organised crime. After his pregnant girlfriend is forced to move away by her father, and he is unable to trace her whereabouts, he crosses paths with a local businessman with links to racketeering. His girlfriend then resurfaces but is firmly entangled with the crime syndicate. When he learns she is in serious trouble he is forced to return from Greece, where he has found new love, to care for the daughter he has never met. He learns he has been left documents by his ex, incriminating various members of the crime organisation. Up against professional hitmen and a crooked police superintendent obstructing investigations, our solicitor persuades police officers and acquaintances of dubious credentials to assist him in ending the organised law breaking so he can return to Greece.

Licensed For Vengeance

Is the sequel to Death Factory where we find our solicitor now married and living an idyllic life on a Greek island. When the drug cartel's assassination attempt on him goes badly wrong and someone close dies instead, he embarks on a mission to find those responsible. To assist with his purpose, he reunites with a clandestine organisation that possesses extraordinary powers and who are taxed with smashing organised crime. But as they close in on the cartel's leadership, the solicitor's daughter is kidnapped in retaliation and his attention becomes focused on finding and rescuing her. Another hard hitting, no nonsense thriller with a twist in the tale.

The Stonemason

Bullied by his elder brother and discovering he is illegitimate; Ross Williams leaves home for London. He joins the police force and ultimately becomes the leader of an armed response unit.

When a drug fuelled youth goes on a shooting spree in a supermarket, Williams' squad is despatched, but with a new leader. However, Williams is forced to assume control which instigates a sequence of events that impacts on the rest of his life.

He leaves the force and eventually returns to his native Northumberland where he inherits a dilapidated estate and title from his real father. Over a period of years he and his wife improve and develop the estate and its many offshoots into thriving businesses, yet, he is bedevilled with the past and the appearance of those who would do him and his family harm, coupled with unavoidable issues that continuously arise to test his resolve.

Printed in Great Britain
by Amazon